William Pullar, a retired local and national journalist with some 50 years of experience, was a crime writer who covered many headline-grabbing news items between the 1970s and the 2000s. Now retired, he enjoys recalling the characters he met in his heyday.

To Jessica, whose undying support enabled this tale to be told.

William Pullar

HEIST DENIAL

AUSTIN MACAULEY PUBLISHERS™

LONDON · CAMBRIDGE · NEW YORK · SHARJAH

A CIP catalogue record for this title is available from the British Library.

ISBN 9781528985451 (Paperback)
ISBN 9781528985468 (Hardback)
ISBN 9781528985475 (ePub e-book)

www.austinmacauley.com

First Published 2024
Austin Macauley Publishers Ltd®
1 Canada Square
Canary Wharf
London
E14 5AA

To Joanna, whose undying support, patience and loyalty has enabled this story to be told.

Also, Marlowe for providing support and comments.

To Glynis, for ideas and suggestions.

Lastly, thanks to the *Cannae Sutra* by Rupert Besley for the Scottish ditties, published by Birlinn Limited.

To understand the slang of the day used by underworld communities, turn to the glossary at the end of the book.

The History

THE THREE, well-dressed elderly men, stood around the grave, waiting for the stonemason to complete installing the gravestone for their friend Reg. Each found their minds re-living their adventures with him, they were remembering his fondness for miniature poodles and military hardware.

Self-styled 'Colonel', Guy Granger, South Londoner Lenny Smith and John 'Jock' Mackenzie stood by the grave and saw the newly erected tombstone for their departed fellow 'blagger' and long-time friend, Reg Crowther and nodded in appreciation.

When together as one gang, they had spent most of their adult life as 'guests' of the British penal system, mainly due to their inept attempts at robberies. However, a folk law had grown up around their blunders. To some, they were misunderstood heroes fighting injustices of the State, to others a quad of criminal buffoons. Criminologist, studying the criminals mind and why certain types teamed up, were baffled why the original Gang of Four had for many years been firm friends. When Reg died, the suggestion was because they all shared the same birthdate–Friday, February 13–in different years. On their release, the colonel would plan another 'perfect' robbery that would make them rich. Their idyll never came to fruition.

They stood around the grave and remembered the past and their newly found desire to be 'honest and hard-working'.

After the ceremony, the three, now called themselves 'The Trio', all inept bank robbers, who had spent most of their adult life serving jail sentences after robbing banks or post offices for which they were always caught and faced trial. They adjourned to their local, the *Gripe and Groan*, in the South Coast town of Bogwash-by-the-Sea. In a rare break from his usual tipple of Flowers Bitter, the man calling himself colonel, sipped the second double measure of Glenfiddich whisky and began reminiscing fondly on the several visits which Reg had paid him whilst he was at Shepton Mallet as a young adventurous conscript airman.

Jock, to whom understandable English language was a complete mystery, grunted in his barely comprehensible mixture of Glasgow slang, Gaelic and English, designed to confuse. Friends commented, "Surprised he made it past the Military Police guards," whenever he visited the man yet to call himself colonel.

Lenny, whose teenage sojourn in a 1960s' Borstal had not benefited his education, chimed in, "But, he learned a lot more in Wormwood Scrubs than I did."

The colonel looked around guardedly before saying quietly, "The Scrubs days were good."

The landlord shook his head when he saw the three and told the barmaid he was going to his club to enjoy a round of golf, he couldn't cope with the Trio.

As the three swopped stories of their past heists and jail terms, they were joined by local police sergeant Craig Wallace. He is one of few who knew the background of the three men and that of the late Reg, he ordered a pint and joined them, uninvited, and began referring to their real past until interrupted by the formidable Martha Samuels, in pursuit of Jock. She had declared her love for the Scotsman and had once chased him, barefooted, along Brighton seafront from a concert venue, much to the bemusement of passers-by, shouting her love for the Highlander Jock who was carrying his bagpipes and dressed in full highland regalia whilst Martha was decked-out in a flamboyant and risqué costume, complete with a large bonnet made of Ostrich feathers, as a member of the dance troupe, 'The Tartanettes'.

All chatter about 'The Trio's' background came to a halt as Martha came into the pub; she had seen the three enter the boozer and came to remind Jock that he was due at a dress rehearsal of the Tartanettes Burlesque dancers the next day. He confirmed he'd be at the church hall of St Jasper's with his bagpipes and wearing his highland gear.

Jock Mackenzie, 78, was now enjoying his new career accompanying their stage routine alongside the five-man rock and roll band, dressed in gorilla costumes, Guy and the Gorillas.

Lenny Smith, 77, was delighted with his new occupation as the mini-bus driver for the burlesque dancers.

Early, the following morning, the self-styled 'Colonel' Guy Granger, 81, walked along the footpath of the River Boggy, he was considering offers he'd been given to talk about his adventurous life along with a book idea. He made his way home to the council owned and run, Retreat Residential Home to meet up with his two pals.

This was now their home after they had been released early, two years before, from their last incarceration in one of Her Majesty's 'Holiday Homes'. It still irritated the colonel that they'd spent time banged-up and they hadn't been involved in any robbery, simply training others to rob without violence, ensuring their pupils received the best heisting education. The trial judge hadn't been impressed.

On the day Reg died, his three pals were facing a Crown Court trial following the failed robbery on a closed-down post office. It had been deemed that Reg was unfit to plead, the remaining three had pleaded guilty of attempting to rob the post office, dressed in gorilla costumes wearing hi-viz jackets and garish Bermuda shorts, attempting to get convicted and be given a sentence that would return them to a world they understood. The judge, Sir Guy Carrington-Worth had a sense of humour and gave them a two-year suspended sentence and called them a bunch of buffoons. The Judge confiscated the gorilla costumes which were to feature in the future of a disbanded rock band, newly reformed.

Now, a few months after Reg's death, the remaining members of The Gang of Four were coming to terms with living in the outside world and complying with the terms of the legacy that Reg had left them.

They were coping with idiosyncratic events and other octogenarian tenants at the Retreat Residential Home in English South Coast at town of Bogwash-by-the-Sea. To them their fellow tenants, council and private, were weird, anti-social misfits, whether rich or poor.

All three avoided the attention of widows from 'The Retreat' and certain members of the Tartanettes Burlesque group. They managed to convince police of their innocence whenever a heist was undertaken by a mystery band of elderly men. One detective was convinced they were, in fact, the old

Gang of Four and Reg was still alive and in hiding to confuse the law. They had, by accident, created impeachable alibis.

Colonel Guy Granger continued his after dinner speaking enterprise and penning his memoires as an unsuccessful 'blagger'. The number of his after-dinner speeches grew, publishers showed interest in his book, *'Confessions of a bank robber'*.

Lenny's efforts to talk 'proper' were reaping rewards, he'd begun to lose much of his South London patois and replaced by his version of an educated speech patter, no one believed anyone spoke this way. Sadly, his overall intelligence level showed little sign of improvement and his efforts to chat-up 'totty', were still failing and he enjoyed being the mini-bus driver for the Tartanettes.

Jock was delighted with being a kilted piper and piano accordion player for the group of middle-age Burlesque dancers and be the centre of attraction for a section of their high-kicking dance routine. He did his best to avoid Martha Samuels, fellow Retreat resident and one of the dance troupe's line-up, who had declared her love for him.

Throughout his criminal career, he'd confused police and courts with his strange mangled language, he claimed was Gaelic. It was to be some years before it was exposed as a strange mix of different dialects along with what had become recognised as gobbledygook, some Glaswegian slang and English. This strange mixture usually prevented clashes and confused Scottish Sherriff's and later English judges by claiming he didn't understand what the police and courts were saying. Despite his efforts, he still spent time relishing in a 'holiday camp', restricting his freedom.

The tartan clad Tartanettes had become popular, along with the re-formed 1960s' pop group, Guy and the Gorillas. Following a few successful shows in the provinces, a TV company were planning a Saturday night variety show, reminiscent of the 1950s and 1960s, featuring the high-stepping dancers, a lone piper, giving musical support and a gorilla costume clad rock band along with other acts of the period. The proposed show had already been dubbed 'The Geriatrics'.

One of the 'respectable' lady residents of the Retreat was retired English language teacher Joanna Creswell who delighted in chastising 'stupid' men who constantly made mistakes with their language courses. She had lost her last teaching post at a secondary modern school because of her over use of the cane. She frequently campaigned for the return of the use of the cane or the leather strap in education. She had a collection of rulers, canes and leather straps she called her 'Museum of Punishment'. Which 'tool' she would use, depended on the 'idiocy factor' of each 'pupil'.

Fellow residents had no idea what her chosen 'retirement hobby' consisted of. Gossip convinced many she gave English lesson for the older men and their smiling faces, as they were leaving, were appreciation of her teaching skills. She hadn't yet realised that some of her language students were really men who enjoyed being spanked. Her activities had come to the notice of a Brighton-based 'professional' chastisement group, SOBS, the Brighton 'Society of Brighton Spankers'. They had tried to bring her into the 'professional' fold and failed. She claimed her activities were for educational purposes only.

She was once an English language teacher who had been banned from the classrooms following a scandal involving over use of the cane on a boy's backsides. She specialised in chastising students who made mistakes with their English lessons. She now gave lessons, and punishment, to mature male students. She didn't charge them for the punishment she gave them when they fouled-up their lessons.

Other Retreat residents had little idea that one of their fellow former tenants was a retired chief constable who wandered naked around his flat and claimed that anyone walking down a nearby lane to the sea, was a housebreaker on the prowl. His son was the assistant chief of Bogshire police with a predilection for doing as little as possible.

Most members of the force and others had forgotten his name when he quietly retired to Weymouth after the debacle of his crashed police car in a garden pond and being battered by an elderly lady house owner. He organised a residential home for his father along the coast in Swanage, a former chief constable of a West Country force who had lost his job due to mismanagement some years before. He believed his 'secret policeman' activities in Bogwash were an important part of crime solving. Bogshire police chiefs thought otherwise.

At least he was no longer a problem for the Bogwash police and the management of the Retreat. The local police were pleased they didn't have to respond to his various allegations of criminal activity by dog walkers and courting couples in the lane outside the Retreat, all proving wrong.

Many private parties were held to celebrate the ACC and his father's departure from Bogwash. They didn't get an invite to one. On moving home, he promptly annoyed the local constabulary by claiming local Dorset crab and lobster fishermen were drug smugglers.

The eighty-five-year old's ambition was to return to Bogwash and help their crime fighting. Meanwhile, he would show the Dorset force his investigative skills. He'd watched two small boats leave the small Dorset port in the hope the pots they'd laid down a couple of days before would hold a good haul. From his harbour-side retirement home, he saw them return without a crab or lobster in sight. In his mind, the fishermen were up to no good. He wanted to ingratiate himself with Dorset police. He failed.

Rastafarian drug dealer, Sonny Summerton had been let out of prison under licence before the Gang of Four became tenants at the Retreat. He'd been warned about his previous activities and told he had to keep clear of crime involving growing and selling drugs. He ignored this 'guidance' and promptly returned to his old ways and re-established contacts with his druggy friends. Although, not a tenant of the Retreat he had rented the greenhouse and vegetable plot.

His drug growing and dealing empire came to an explosive end, thanks to the colonel's dislike of drug dealers. Before undertaking the gorilla clad attempted robbery, the colonel had poured petrol over the cannabis plants to destroy them. Summerton had lit a 'spliff' and threw the still alight match, into the vapour-soaked interior of the greenhouse. As he took a drag on his cannabis cigarette, an explosion and fire ruined his crop of cannabis and destroyed the greenhouse. He survived, thanks to a visiting nurse who tended to his burns and doused his ruined Rastafarian dreadlocks. Summerton spent some time in the psychiatric wing of a local hospital and received plastic surgery following the explosion.

Bemoaning the loss of his prized dreadlocks and the ruined cannabis plants, he was eventually returned to jail having broken his early release conditions. He was now facing further drug related charges. The greenhouse at the Retreat remained a smoke blackened, glass-less wreck following the explosion and fire. Summerton tried to claim damages through the Retreat's insurance. The insurance company wrote to him saying his attempts to get compensation would make a good comedy show for television and told him not to bother them again or they would support the council for a claim of compensation for the destroyed greenhouse. The council managed to get compensation from him and planned on replacing the greenhouse.

Lawyers rubbed their hands in glee at the fees they would receive for challenging the council's decision to cancel his contract for the vegetable patch. He was claiming the return of his rental fees that had been paid in advance and any profits of the vegetables that were harvested and sold. It was to be some months before this case came before a judge who said any money that he was due should be donated to any anti-drug or rehabilitation charities.

The convicted drug dealer began to plan his escape from Boggy Moore Prison and retrieve belongings and cash he said he was owed. His efforts would be left suspended.

At the beginning of their second year, and the first of their suspended sentence, living in the Bogwash residential home the Trio made every effort to avoid mixing with other tenants. Among this mix were some newcomers such as the new warden, Stella Stern, who tried to impose her management style but couldn't cope with the idiosyncratic pressures of the

Retreat. Her attempts to bring some discipline had given her, she claimed, a nervous breakdown.

The management returned her to the Retreat after each short stay in the psychiatric wing of the local hospital. Only for her to return, in less than a month, and resume her secretive method of management.

When challenged about their decision to keep sending her back, the council said they would rather send a half-looney back to do her best, than no warden at all.

The Trio had adopted a 'denial programme'. Whenever anyone raised the saga of the bungled post office raid, the colonel was quick to reply that nothing was taken, so he thought they couldn't be charged with theft. His usual response was "Heist, what heist?" Nor would he discuss the two-year suspended prison sentence the three were serving for their failed attempt; he was embarrassed by the 'soft option sentence'. He was also anxious not to break Reg's inheritance conditions. In the first period, they had little contact with fellow tenants, their probation officer attempted several schemes to get them to socialise. So far, a failure.

Elsewhere in the Retreat, there were secret romances, plans to escape a planned marriage, a 'ghost' and newcomers who were not who they seemed to be. A strange mixture of elderly women, some looking for new husbands, lonely men, not knowing what they wanted.

The Trio avoided any criminal activity. The colonel worked on his memories as the 'brains' behind many armed raids and giving talks to an amused legal fraternity.

Lenny continued enjoying acting as the mini-bus driver for the Tartanettes and the band. Jock played his bagpipes and accordion with enthusiasm.

In the nearby parish church of St Jasper's, the diminutive vicar encouraged the efforts of the campanology group. Animals within earshot became used to the clanging, those in the zoo remained in their cages and pens. When the group began their bell ringing, animals in the town, domestic, farm and zoo, fled some miles away to avoid the cacophony.

The noise the group made faded into insignificance with the cacophony of the bellowing of his three-month-old twin boys. Their equally diminutive mother believed the noise was important for the twin's development.

She told family and friends, she didn't miss being the warden at the Retreat as the residents were either loons or ex-cons.

The Brighton gay community were beginning to meet the challenge of pulling the right bell.

Anyone looking at this scene would believe the Retreat was a social idyll. WRONG!

Chapter 1

THE TRIO sat in the bar of The *Gripe and Groan*, formerly, The Talbot, enjoying their daily alcohol intake. The new landlord had changed the name to reflect the number of customers who constantly griped about social issues or groaned about their spouse's latest 'rules' about meeting their friends. No one had exchanged a word for nearly ten minutes. Finally, the colonel spoke up, "Doesn't seem the same without Reg. Quite miss the old blighter."

Lenny took a swig of his beer, giving his best lugubrious, hangdog look and added, "Yeah, its bin three months. He was fun t'have on a blaggin. D'yer remember that time he got his finger stuck in the trigger guard of the shotgun. He always wore those thick gloves, no fingerprints, he would say. He tried to get his figure out and he pulled the trigger by accident and blew a hole in an armchair instead of the ceilin'. God, that wuz a laff'."

The colonel stroked his moustache and rubbed his broken nose, the result of colliding with a van after a failed robbery of a Balham bank. He sat with his chin resting on his two forefingers, sighed and added, "Yeah, if he didn't wear those thick gloves that wouldn't have 'appened, that screw-up was at that exclusive bank in the West End. As I remember, it was the only place we raided and the ceilin' tiles survived. Didn't 'alf make a mess of that manager's chair, thank God no one wuz sittin' in it. Could 'ave been a murder rap." He shook his head.

Lenny added, "Wasn't bankin' on two cop cars and a mini bus parked outside, fourteen tooled-up fuzz on a trainin' exercise nicked us. Didn't stand a chance."

Jock nodded and rubbed his hands through his mop of ginger hair and took a sip of whisky, adding, "Ay, he was fussy, he wouldn't sit in the back of the getaway car. He insisted he sat in the front passenger seat. Then he would tell me which way to drive away from the blaggin." Jock sipped his whisky. His speech pattern was becoming understandable, he was beginning to lose his strange mixture of Glaswegian, Gaelic and English. He remembered an embarrassing incident at one bank robbery.

"We waited for ages because the bank was so busy. Lenny had been fiddling with his belt–nerves, I guess. Suddenly, he shouted, 'Let's go' and we charged into the bank. There were lots of customers, mainly wimmen, as usual we made lots of noise and threatened everyone. Reg's gloved finger got stuck in the trigger guard of 'is sawn-off, as he pulled it free, the gun went off, the pellets smashed a glass-fronted notice on the wall. Most of the wimmen fell about laughin' when his trousers fell-down, he wasn't wearing underpants and was quite aroused with the excitement of the raid. Me recollection is, that we ran out of the bank, with Reg trying to hold 'is trousers up and carrying 'is gun. As I remember, the cash haul was less than a grand. We got nicked three days later. That raid got us a ten-year sentence, and Lenny should have faced a further charge trial of exposing 'imself. He didn't half get some crude comments in the slammer, some of those that couldn't be repeated in company, 'give us a flash' or 'pull yer trousers up', were just a couple of the milder ones. He took the ribbing in good spirit. After that, we persuaded him to wear underpants, a belt and use thin rubber gloves on a heist to avoid leavin' 'is fingerprints."

The colonel sighed and said slowly, "If he'd listened to doctors and m'self to stay off the booze, he might well be alive today." He took a gulp of beer.

Lenny, not known for his intellectual ability, asked, "How come drink caused his problems? He enjoyed his drink, it usually cheered him up."

"Maybe, but it eventually killed him. It was something they call Central Pontine Myelinolysis, sometimes called Osmotic Demyelination," the colonel added, with an air of authority, and was about to give more information when Lenny interrupted.

"Why do they give these tongue-twistin' names to things?"

"It's Latin," the colonel responded.

Lenny looked baffled and downed the last of his pint. "All done in a foreign lingo, so we don't un'erstand," he commented.

Jock stood up, picked up the three empty glasses and proposed he made a rare purchase of their drinks. As he was about to leave for the bar, he quietly said, "Never mind the fancy foreign names. Reg is still dead."

Back at the Retreat, three new tenants were settling in. Belinda Bennett, a wealthy merchant banker's widow and mystery-man, Henry Styles, both in the private wing. In the social wing, was Brenda Bates a retired, one-time, publican who coped with day-to-day problems with the aid of Bell's whisky.

Long-term residents, 'Lady' Anne Pritchard, a former owner of a Brighton 'gentleman's' club and Harold Pearson were still planning their wedding. He had developed a nervous twitch and was plotting an escape route. He wasn't really listening to his fiancée as she told him of the contents of the wedding feast. A one-time manager of the local branch of a large banking group, he'd been retired after an audit showed he'd refused every loan application for ten years and the branch was losing customers and facing closure. He'd been a satisfied customer at Anne's club for many years.

As a life-long confirmed bachelor, the grey haired 76-year-old had become terrified of the idea of being a married man. Although, he'd proposed to Anne following consumption of six large glasses of vintage port, he was now having second thoughts, the main one being, how he was going to enjoy his disappearance to the Caribbean, all he had to do was renew his passport, without Anne realising what he was planning.

Joanna Creswell was saying goodbye to her latest 'English language' pupil who was wincing and rubbing his backside. Known as JJ, the well-spoken gent had been very naughty boy by deliberately failing his language exam and had been punished. Inside the flat, Joanna put her heavy cane back in its display cabinet and chose a lighter, more flexible, one and waited for her next pupil; she knew he liked the sharper 'sting' it inflicted. She knew he was going to be punished, he always muddled up his English exam. Joanna had developed a 'kindness' by allowing clients to choose the punishment they wanted. Her clients enjoyed this arrangement. Despite her age and teaching experience, she hadn't yet realised her clients messed up lessons, just so they were punished. No women attended her lessons. The head of the music department of the local private school was delighted with his 'lesson' as he headed back to take his afternoon class. He'd insisted she play a CD-disc of the Royal Philharmonic Orchestra playing their version of Colonel Bogey whilst thrashing him to disguise his joyful cries of the inflicted pain. He gently rubbed his posterior, pleased that the lesson had 'hit the right note'.

Joanna watched him walk up the road, trying to understand why an educated man deliberately made mistakes, just so he could be punished. Most odd. She couldn't work out what the men were up to, would she ever understand them?

To the rest of the tenants in the Retreat, life went on as usual, unaware at the havoc being wreaked. The newly elected Peoples Freedom Party on Bogwash Council had little idea about the management of a small borough and civil servants were leaving in droves. Psychiatrists and other mental health specialists were kept busy, overwhelmed with counselling requests from the two types of tenancies at the Retreat. Politicians soon learned that activities and solutions at the Retreat were best 'swept under the carpet'; a style of management in which the Freedom Party would become 'skilled'. Those in the Housing Department responsible for dealing with the Retreat, avoided any contact.

The two types of tenancies at the Retreat and those who remained, led to strange alliances and conflicts. On one side, the private wing housed wealthy widows and widowers, who believed they should have preferential treatment.

In the 'social' wing, there were those who needed help with affordable accommodation and living expenses paid for by the state. In addition, the local council encouraged a policy, in association with the prison authorities, of housing long-term prisoners released from their sentence. The Trio fell into this category.

The reality was, the residents ran affairs, with Martha Samuels acting as Chair for the Resident's Management Committee.

Any council workmen assigned to carry out repairs, did so in pairs, with a burly security guard to protect them from angry tenants demanding their repairs take precedence. Care workers assigned to give daily help to invalid tenants would only attend in pairs, one of them, the largest available. In the previous two years, six council officials and wardens had been committed to hospital suffering from a variety of mental conditions they blamed on the Retreat.

The colonel told his probation officer, prison was a more peaceful and understandable environment than the Retreat, "Full of looneys, it is."

Chapter 2

THE TRIO remained quiet about Reg's bequest and their plans for the remaining months of their suspended sentence. The colonel stood in his flat and read a letter from Angela Cowley, once one of Reg's former team of carers, now living in America. Her son, James, now ten, had been diagnosed with autism by English doctors, when aged five. American specialists said he was suffering from Pandas Syndrome. The English system had, allegedly, appeared to do little to help his condition. None of the three knew Reg had funded the trip to the States for James to get another medical assessment. Before Reg died, he'd left the boy a bequest in his will. None of the Trio were aware of this.

Angela had attended his funeral and agreed to keep in touch with the colonel and let him know how James was progressing. In the letter, Angela said he was improving and doing well at school and settling into the American way of life.

He pushed the letter inside his jacket pocket. "I'll read it properly later. I wonder what Pandas Syndrome is? I must find out," he muttered to himself as he picked up his walking stick. He said goodbye to Minnie, leaving her preening her long ginger hair and headed for the lounge to read that day's edition of the Daily Mail whilst waiting for Jock and Lenny, and their daily trip to the *Gripe and Groan* pub.

Apartments in the block frequently became available due to residents moving home or getting the tenancy of a wooden box and a permanent slot in a cemetery.

As the colonel waited for his two pals, a tall, well-dressed, elderly man, wearing a cravat, came in and sat down. He asked the colonel, "You live here?"

"I stay here, yes."

"I'm Henry Styles, I moved in yesterday, pleasant place, I must say."

"Colonel Granger." Before he could say any more, Henry Styles pulled a long Havana cigar from his top jacket pocket and a pair of clippers from a side pocket. He looked around for an ashtray.

The colonel coughed. "This is a non-smoking lounge." He pointed to several small signs saying, 'No Smoking.'

Henry Styles twiddled the cigar between his fingers, frowned, then pushed the cigar back into his pocket asking, "Does this place have a smoking lounge?"

"No smoking anywhere," the colonel replied.

At this point Lenny and Jock entered the lounge.

The colonel stood up and said, "These two are Lenny and Jock, they also live here. Like me, they don't smoke."

He turned to the pair and said, "This is Henry Styles, he moved in yesterday and he smokes."

"You're a strange lot," Styles commented.

Showing little interest in saying more to the new man, the colonel said, "C'mon lads, we have a social meeting to go to."

On their way to the pub, the colonel said, "There's summit about that geezer, that ain't right?"

"Like what?" Lenny asked.

"Not sure."

Jock added, "But you hardly spoke to him."

The colonel tapped the side of his nose with his forefinger, "Just instinct, just instinct." The three walked on.

Back at the Retreat, Belinda walked into the lounge carrying a light walking cane and sat down. Henry Styles watched the widow with interest and opened the conversation. "Well, hello, my dear. Let me introduce myself, I'm Henry Styles, I've just moved in." He stroked his moustache and took out his cigar from his top pocket and rolled it between his fingers.

Belinda gave him a haughty look and said, "Can't you see the signs. This is a no smoking lounge." She stood up, gave him an unsmiling look and walked out of the lounge.

Henry Styles re-pocketed the cigar, pursed his lips and nodded.

In the background, the bells of St Jaspers rang out. The cacophony of sound had much improved. The bats remained hanging from the rafters, domestic animals stayed at home, the dairy herds delivered their milk. At the zoo, the animals were content to stay in their cages, they were all getting used to the noise. The diminutive vicar encouraged members of the Brighton gay community to pull the right ropes and enjoy the bell-ringing experience. They were showing great improvement. He remembered how, when the bell-ringing group was formed, bats, zoo animals and domestic animals fled the town.

As the bells rang, a man of military bearing was leaving the Retreat, he re-arranged his trilby hat, then rubbed his posterior and strode up the road with a smile on his face. Major Peter Hopkins liked a bit of discipline.

Joanna had poured herself a small sherry and was watching her new client walking up the road. She muttered to herself, "What makes a man like that come to me, gets his language screwed-up and enjoyed being chastised with a caning across his bum? Very strange."

The colonel ordered a round of drinks in *The Gripe and Groan* and reiterated his belief that something was amiss with the new man called Styles. "I think we'll have to watch him very carefully, there's summat odd about him," he said, as he sipped his pint of bitter. The other two were more interested in their drinks and other customers than the colonel's concerns.

In her private flat at the Retreat, Belinda Bennett made a phone call, when she finished. She smiled and made herself a cup of coffee.

Lenny had, from his young days, been described as educationally backward. The prison authorities described him as intellectually challenged. Many described him as a Cockney, without savvy.

His childhood and teenage days were spent in Wandsworth, long before it became yuppy territory. He was frequently called 'thick'.

Any lady with a 'classy' accent was a target for his feeble and embarrassing attempts to woo them 'to bed'. As he became older, his efforts became more comical and always led to rebuttal, sometimes leaving him with a black eye or a painful groin. Such was his intellectual level that he never considered it was his sometimes crude efforts that often led to a lady giving him a reminder that he was 'out of order'. He usually blamed his black eye on an open kitchen cupboard door.

On one occasion, an elderly title lady chastised him by a well-aimed kick to the groin, telling him she hoped it would to improve his manners.

He believed well known, male or female, TV or movie stars were either moonlighting as prison guards, probation officers, council staff, carers or were temporary tenants of the private wing of the Retreat whilst 'resting'. This frequently led to laughter and ridicule which led him into many rows, claiming he had 'inside knowledge'. This usually resulted in Lenny ending up in an argument. The colonel, Jock and the late Reg would often have to rescue him from a fight.

Using his secret inside 'information' he claimed new tenant Belinda Bennett was in fact a well-known actress retired from her acting career and her real name was Josie Lumsden. Lenny wouldn't expand on his 'knowledge', simply saying he wanted to honour her obvious desire to retire in secret.

The colonel and Jock shook their heads, having experienced his bizarre claims before, usually with comical results.

Chapter 3

A FEW days later, the colonel caught a train to Reading Station then changed platforms and travelled to Bristol to talk to a group of lawyers, both Crown Prosecution and private. On the journey, he continued to ponder the background of Styles and what Belinda Bennett's background was before she married.

At the Bristol hotel, he was pleased to see a packed hall. His talk today was about, ***The Art of Harmless Robbery and Failed Heists***. The colonel vehemently believed a robbery, where no one was hurt, was the sign of a good professional.

Following a lunch, he began telling his tale, after a few jokes and complaining that there was no pension scheme for blaggers. Nor did the taxman bother them for unearned income after they had been nicked, after all they hadn't benefitted from the proceeds of the crime. The audience seemed to warm to his tales of villainy.

"I will tell you about those I've trained and trips to rob smaller banks in country towns, away from our usual haunts.

"Some years ago, I saw a unique business opportunity until the courts closed my enterprise down and I was sent down for five years, my three other directors were banged-up as well. We were found guilty of conspiracy to rob, it seems it was the only charge they could pin on us. It was to be the last prison sentence we were to serve. What was galling, we had paid tax on our profits. Now, you are asking, what was this great idea that we lost out on?"

The colonel was interrupted when a voice in the audience shouted. "Go on, surprise us."

"And tell you, I will," he responded.

"I'd formed a company called 'Heist Away'. The idea was to give aspiring young blaggers a good grounding in the art of being a successful robber without 'urtin' anyone."

The audience laughed.

"The fact that we got nicked every time we did a blaggin' was sheer bad luck, not bad plannin'. We held the view if you're goin' to do it, do it the right way."

A voice from the back of the audience shouted, "Ever heard of self-kidology?"

The rest of the audience clapped and laughed. This appeared to have woken up two snoring elderly men who promptly clapped as the room went quiet not knowing why they were responding. The colonel ignored the interruption.

"We soon had many pupils, young and old, even a couple of young women and a matronly type. They all paid our fees in advance, we thought we'd made it.

"We taught them how to nick the right type of getaway car, we preferred the tried and trusty Jaguar Mark Two. A great car.

"We taught them how to use a sawn-off shotgun properly and how to hide it in yer jacket, trousers or sports bag. Women preferred a bag. They didn't like sawn-offs stick down their knickers and tights it reminded them of unwanted male attention."

There was a ripple of laughter.

"We provided details of armourers who would hire us the guns and ammo and take them back when used and make them disappear. Any evidence we had used a shooter was lost.

"We had a legal team consisting of…"

He paused and looked around the room, then continued, "A QC, noted for his aggressive courtroom interrogation techniques, taught students how to combat police questioning and legal etiquette. We also had a lawyer, who'd been convicted of fraud and struck off, he knew every devious trick in the book. They were well paid." The audience clapped and cheered. This woke up the two elderly men who had fallen sleep again.

"We were doing very well. I broke with tradition and bought a six litre Mercedes for cash. My three pals bought similar vehicles. We were on a high and in our view earning an 'onest livin' and payin' tax. You'd be surprised how many wanted to join our classes. As far as we were concerned we were training students to do a heist in a responsible manner.

"It came to an end when the cops raided us. The former lawyer was giving a talk on how to deal with being arrested. We didn't shop the QC, he's still active in the court circuit, I won't say which one."

The audience cheered and clapped as they looked around. "No, he's not here, he works another circuit," the colonel added. He went onto to say, "We'll take a break now and allow you to re-charge yer glasses. I'll talk about the robberies that went wrong afterwards.

After fifteen minutes, the audience resumed their seats and the colonel re-started his talk, "Ladies and gentlemen, no amount of detailed planning ensured our escape route was the best. Let me tell you of where one raid I'd planned everything in fine detail. The great unknown was the weather, the damned English weather. In our usual style we blew a hole in the ceiling of the bank and fled the scene with a holdall full of cash. No one got hurt. To me, physically hurting customers or staff was a no-no."

The audience cheered. Then someone shouted, "What was your regiment in the army, colonel?"

"Never served in the army wuz in the army, served time as an erk doin' national service in the RAF. No, I gave m'self the title colonel and it stuck."

"Anyway, back to my story. I had planned, what I thought, was the perfect getaway route. I hadn't planned on the effects of two days of rain hitting the Cotswolds and particularly near Cheltenham. We raced down a Gloucestershire back lane in our stolen Jaguar. We came around a bend at speed and ran slap bang into a raging torrent of water crossing the road. When I'd cased the route, it was a small dribble of a stream. Jock couldn't stop the car in time and we were washed down stream, sideways, until stopped by a fallen tree. The car became tangled in the branches, which prevented us from sinking or getting out. None of us wanted to try and wade ashore, even if we could open a door. All we got were wet feet as the water seeped into the car.

"The rain eased off after a couple of hours when we were spotted by a farmer looking for stranded sheep. It took the fire brigade and hour to get to us. We were rescued and taken to hospital. Then ended up in the local nick. We later discovered we had managed to blag around one hundred and twenty thousand, which was later recovered from the car. It was one of our best hauls of cash throughout our enterprise years. We never got to spend a penny of it and did a seven-years of a ten-year stretch in choky for our efforts."

The audience laughed and clapped.

Back in Bogwash Lenny was taking English diction lessons from Miss Creswell. She never caned him even though he bungled several phrases. Joanna made a pot of tea for them and chatted about the stupidity of the Council. She told a friend she didn't punish him because his speech problems were genuine, and she quite liked him.

He was determined to improve his speech and use 'proper' words and rid himself of his South London patois. He had so far failed in his attempts to chat-up a better class of 'skirt', his usual speech pattern had become mixed with a Thames Estuary accent.

Jock was in a Bogwash hall practicing his bagpiping skills at a rehearsal with the Tartanettes and the rock and roll band, Guy and the Gorillas.

In a pub in Oxford City centre, four men sat and planned their next blagging. One said, "Got the cops baffled, they think the gang of four are still active, but can't prove it."

The others laughed. They finished their drinks and headed for their various homes in the area.

In Bogwash, it was early evening, the colonel had returned from Bristol, the Trio moved from The *Gripe and Groan* to another pub in town.

The colonel sat silently for a few minutes then said, "The cops think we're involved in these four handed robberies and Reg is in hiding somewhere."

Lenny laughed, "Yeah, in a wooden box, six-foot under."

Jock took a sip of whisky. "What we gonna do aboot these four pretending to be us?" he asked, in understandable English in a Scottish dialect.

"I'll think of summut," the colonel said quietly. "I'll think of summut."

He returned home to find Minnie waiting for him and demanding food.

"Minnie, old dear we've gotta find out who these guys are. The cheeky beggars are copying our style. At least we can prove we weren't involved. For once we've got good alibis."

Minnie meowed as if thanking him for the evening meal, then settled down on the settee. After making himself supper he sat with Minnie. He chatted out loud, "I've got to find out who these mobsters are, they're making us targets." Minnie flicked her tail and shut her eyes even tighter, it was if she was wishing he'd leave her to sleep. The colonel added, "I should know more about that new woman Bennett and that fella Styles. Come on, let's go to bed."

Minnie suddenly woke up, meowed, then followed him into the bedroom.

Chapter 4

AMONG newcomers at the Retreat was Henry Styles he was a tall and some women would say a handsome, 70-year-old man. He had an air of confidence about him. When out in the street he was rarely seen without a Havana cigar in his mouth. He said he was a semi-retired investment banker still looking for potential investors.

The colonel, and a few other residents were suspicious of him from the outset. He was sitting in the lounge when the Trio arrived at the front door on their way to the morning snifter at the *Gripe and Groan*. They managed to sneak out without meeting him.

At the same time in a busy high street in South London a postmaster sat quietly behind the counter reading the local weekly newspaper. He looked up and saw three, apparently, old men each pointing sawn-off shotguns at him, their faces obscured by masks. He went to press the silent alarm connected to the police station. One man said, "Don't, if yer wanna stay alive, just hand over the cash."

One of the three grabbed the bag of cash and fled the building, the postmaster failed to see how they departed the scene. There was no CCTV operating in the area. It was later discovered £11,000 had been stolen. Details of the robbery were circulated to London and Home County police forces giving scant details of the raid.

As the robbery was underway a retired businessman reported his prize red Mark 2 Jaguar had been stolen overnight from his home in Croydon.

Just before midnight, on the day of the robbery, an annoyed resident of a house in a cul-de-sac in Staines reported a red Jaguar was blocking his driveway. Police soon established it was the stolen car, witnesses confirmed a red car was seen driving away from the South London post office at speed.

Some residents of the street claimed they saw four elderly men leave the Jaguar and get into a large black 4-wheel drive BMW and drive away. No one took its registration.

This robbery was the sixth in over a month. To those who study the history of the underworld these series of heists had the hallmarks of the methods used by the legendary, inept, Gang of Four. Even down to the make of the getaway car. The only problem was, they were stealing money and not being caught. It was the only part that failed to fit the Gang of Four's legendary style.

The next day in Bournemouth the colonel was at the back end of a talk to a seminar of lawyers, basically a repeat of his Bristol offering. Lenny was taking an English diction lesson from Joanna Creswell. Jock sat in The *Gripe and Groan* nursing a large malt whisky waiting for Lenny to finish his lesson and the colonel's return.

The Trio were unaware of the blagging until seeing scant details in the next day's edition of the **Evening Standard**, that someone had discarded on a train, the paper then found its way into the *Gripe and Groan*. The colonel read the report on page seven, saying to himself, "Hells bells they've done better than we ever did," and ripped the article out and pocketed it.

Meanwhile, in the Retreat Henry Styles's attempts to ingratiate himself with the women from both the private and social wings were not making the headway he wanted. Some thought he was charming, others steered clear of him.

Belinda Bennett observed his activities she then returned to her flat and made notes.

Chapter 5

A FEW mornings later the colonel was returning from shopping trip in Bogwash and followed a middle aged, balding, well-dressed man into the Retreat and watched as he made his way to Joanna Creswell's flat. He then went to his own flat and found Minnie the cat waiting for him. Nearly an hour had passed when he believed he heard a loud groaning and howling. The colonel thought he could hear a cane striking bare flesh and Joanna telling the client he was a naughty boy and he deserved punishment for the stupid spelling and verbal delivery mistakes.

Eton educated merchant banker, Sir Steven Striker, was pleased with his lesson and had booked another in a week's time. He thanked Joanna and told her it was one of his best investments.

The colonel saw the well-dressed 'student' walking up the road, occasionally stopping and gently rubbing his rear end then getting into a chauffeur-driven Bentley. Little did Joanna guess that her freelance English lessons, including punishment, if the 'student' messed-up the tutorial, would lead to war with SOBS, the Society of Brighton Spankers, a group of ladies, who specialised in inflicting pain for payment on men who wanted to be 'chastised'. The wealthy banker had once been one of their best customers. He now told friends Joanna inflicted a better class of pain at less cost.

Joanna charged for the English lessons but didn't ask for payment from 'pupils' for the caning if they messed up the session. She believed that 'naughty' boys should be punished. No girls had joined her 'classes'. Members of SOBS decided she had to be put out of business as her 'services' cost less than theirs and they were losing trade. Previous attempts to bring her into the mainstream punishment business had failed, they decided that she had be 'persuaded' to stop this side of her lessons. They agreed to send in Clive 'Crackers' Crumb to 'suggest' she retire from the spanking business. He'd earned his nickname with his crazy methods of 'shaking' down anyone who crossed members of SOBS. He'd served a 12-month jail term for inflicting actual bodily harm when he'd strung a customer from a beam in his cottage on behalf of one member of SOBS. A local councillor, he'd refused to pay for her services. Crumb had attached a heavy weight to the man's testicles. The court was told the councillor would never be able to 'rise' again when circumstances beckoned.

Crumb was better known as 'Crackers' and was usually part paid for his 'shake-down' in cash and a hearty backside caning by two of the members at the same time. He enjoyed the arrangement and thought they'd done it perfectly when he couldn't sit down for an hour.

It was late in the afternoon on the same day when the colonel wandered into the communal lounge at the Retreat and found George Goodchild, the retired farmer, trying to entertain the ladies present with his stories of how to milk cows. They showed little interest. They'd heard his tales before. When he finally realised they were ignoring him he tried a new story line.

The colonel sat in a corner only half listening to George. In another corner chair sat newcomer, Belinda Bennett. George began telling of his predatory bull, "He wuz determined to sort out any young heifer and any old cow that came into sight, I mean's the four-legged kind. Rampant he wuz."

One elderly, big town bred, lady fell into the trap. "Sort 'em for what?" she asked.

He paused, looked around furtively and said, "When they be ready, yer know ready, he wuz at ' em. God, he put a new meaning into screwin." He slapped one hand into the crook of his elbow and raised his forearm into the vertical with his fist closed and let a growl like sound.

This was the third time in a few days Belinda had heard the same stories. She stood up, clutching her lightweight walking stick, and strode over to George and said, "You may enjoy telling us of the sex life of a rampant bull and some dozy cows. We don't want to hear it again and again. Now just shut up or I'll sort you out," waving her walking stick at him. "Believe me, I know people who'd deal with you."

Belinda stormed out of the room, leaving George pleading. "What'd I say? What'd I say? I wuz only jokin, I haven't hurt anyone," he asked.

No one answered him or commiserated. He wandered out of the lounge muttering about 'bullyin' women.

The colonel chuckled, he must get to know Belinda. He, like other residents, had little idea of her former career before she married a wealthy businessman.

At this point, a very sober Jock arrived, soon followed by Lenny and the three departed for a visit to the *Gripe and Groan*.

Chapter 6

FOR some months the Retreat had relied on temporary wardens and many had been sectioned under the Mental Health Act and were still 'resting' in Bogwash Mental Hospital. Other simply refused to return to the residential home.

Finally, the council found someone who was prepared to take of the onerous task of managing the residents. Stella Stern had begun working as the new Warden at the Retreat and had been told how difficult some of the residents could be. She told the council she was good at dealing with elderly people and their problems. Little did the 'inmates' realise this short, slim, hyperactive female would be as barmy as the ex-army, female sergeant Fiona Fuller, they had managed to oust the year before.

Miss Stern was also a, 'no nonsense' operator. She preferred minimal contact with the tenants. She kept her office door closed and locked, even when she was on duty. She believed that lack of face-to-face contact with tenants prevented anyone complaining and was the solution to good management.

One of her first innovative ideas was having an electronic communication system installed at the Retreat which enabled her to talk to each resident from the comfort of her office and the tenant to summon help in an emergency. Good thinking, all thought. That was until she began calling residents at six in the morning. Some of the elderly's sleeping habits didn't quite fit into her communication regime. The Council were swamped with complaints. In their usual style no action was taken. To the Council staff the Retreat was regarded as a law unto itself and intervention was futile.

Stern's latest 'brilliant' idea would cause tenants to revolt. With some displaying placards. Tenants believed they could come and go from the Retreat without any formality. Miss Stern thought otherwise. She had implemented a regulation that required all tenants should sign a book saying when they were leaving the building and recording their return.

The scheme lasted barely 24-hours it took the militant tenants committee saying their 'human rights' were to form an action group called Sod Off Too Awful Management, better known by the acronym, SOTAM was formed. This ten-strong group picketed the building with placards declaring such sentiments as:

SOTAM SAYS:
GIVE US
OUR HUMAN
RIGHTS
Or
SOTAM SAYS:
FREEDOM
OF
MOVEMENT

Determined to exploit the SOTAM campaign and publicise her own services. On the second day Joanna Creswell joined other residents displaying a placard and loudly shouting her demands.

On one side was the hand-written slogan:

SPANKING
IS THE
ANSWER
And
MAKE
SPANKING
LEGAL

After a couple a couple of hours members of SOBS joined the demo with placards declaring:

SOBS give
The best
Spanks

Spanking
Is a man's
Right

Legalise
Spanking

A small number of men were seen cheering this demo.

Postmen and deliverymen were prevented from entering the Retreat. The Royal Mail and courier companies thought they could get around the demonstrations by sending female operatives. Wrong. The women had a greater sympathy for the protestors than their male colleagues and either offered to relieve the pickets of their placards while they had a break— a frequent need in many cases—or disappeared, only to return shortly bearing hot drinks and high-fiving everyone on the line.

As the protestors argued among themselves on whether Joanna should be allowed to remain. Whilst others stumbled back and forth with the aid of walking sticks, zimmer frames and wheeled walking aids. A coach from the company, Wally Amos, on an unusual route for a sightseeing tour, pulled up and disgorged a group of some thirty Japanese tourists, who paused to watch the spectacle, taking pictures of a very English octogenarian protest. The group told the operator it had been the most exciting part of the day a few were pleased they had the chance to see English democracy at work. Joanna tried various hand gestures to advertise her services to the male tourists but was met only with looks of considerable bewilderment.

Elderly visitors to St Jaspers' church would soon become part of the crowd supporting the protest. At least thanks to a reporter and cameraman, of the Bogshire Bugle, after a story appeared in the paper about the protest.

Joanna revelled in the publicity and waved her placard at visitors and other curious pedestrians. Martha enjoyed bellowing out anti-council slogans through a mega-phone. Police failed to stop her when she opened the window of her first floor flat and continued her noisy protests and played loud 1960s' rock music to the assembled crowd.

Newspaper, television and radio reporters tried to interview Stella Stern, only to be told she was on sick leave. In between musical arrangements reporters tried to question Martha, they retreated to a safe distance when she threw a bucket of water out of her first-floor window.

Bye-standers could not understand the significance of the spanking element, but press photographers concentrated on Joanna's banners.

The Bugle ran the headline:

ELDERLY AND
SPANKERS IN
JOINT DEMO
RESIDENTS of a Bogwash Council home have joined forces with a language teacher, who spanks naughty pupils, to stop plans by their new warden.

The new group are complaining about plans to reduce their freedom.

The protest leader is said to be Retreat tenant, Martha Samuels, who expounded the views of the group through a mega phone from a first-floor window.

The group claim their protests will continue until these plans stop.

The Bugle are investigating the spanking element of the protests.

The story went on to say the Council were investigating the claims. A large picture of the banner carrying elderly residents, along with Joanna Creswell's lonely message, stood alongside the Bugle story. On reading it Council leaders suddenly decided it was the ideal time to take their holiday entitlement.

Returning, from the pub late that afternoon the colonel, Lenny and Jock managed to force their way through the crowd of spectators and enter the building. Minnie saw them and leaped from the oak tree to the veranda and through the open window. She waited patiently for the colonel, her landlord, to arrive and feed her.

Inside the building members of SOBS agreed who with Joanna's demands were pondering, how they were they going to persuade her to become part of their organisation.

Lenny was in the lounge waiting for the colonel and Jock when Belinda walked in. He looked at her and nodded his head. She said nothing to him. A couple of minutes later Jock arrived soon followed by the colonel. She ignored Jock but acknowledged the colonel. Lenny walked past her to the door and the three departed for their midday trip to the pub.

When the three had sat down with their drinks Lenny was the first to open the conversation, "That new woman, I'm trying to think who she looks like."

"Let us know, when you remember," the colonel replied.

Lenny sat in silence for some minutes when he suddenly said, "I've got it, I've got it."

"Got what?" Jock asked. "Cramp or what?"

"That new woman, I fink it's that woman on the tele, yer know Josie Lumsden."

"Who the hell is that?" the colonel asked.

"The television actress, she's clearly in disguise, doesn't want us to know who she really is now she's retired. Don't worry I'll keep it a secret."

The colonel shook his head and looked at Jock shaking his head, then let out a gentle sigh.

Chapter 7

THE *Gripe and Groan* attracted a strange mixture of drinkers among them the Head of the Department of Social Re-alignment at the University of Bogwash, Professor Robert Rumple, who had already given the University a reputation for unusual, and most certainly, unique courses. They included:

How to be a professional idiot
Idiocy, do it the right way
Responsible idiocy
Idiocy, a form of sanity
Make a career out of idiocy
The art of being a creep
Be a professional creep
Creep your way to success

Most of his students were on day release from prison, mental institutions or referral from psychiatrists. Some students were from local government wanting to learn how to ingratiate themselves with the public and the business community.

The Trio frequently saw him at the *Gripe and Groan* and listened bemused to what they considered his 'off the wall' ideas for adult education.

The Professor's latest objective was to attract more female students to his department. To this end, he recruited the self-styled, psychologist, Celia Worthy to provide new courses, specifically aimed at women. She claimed to have a reputation for innovative thinking and forthright delivery of her views. It hadn't occurred to the professor the problems he was to unleash with her appointment. Her first suggestion for courses were entitled.

Re-training your man.
Training your man to be a managed sex symbol.
How to make your man obedient.

Celia had been married four times and believed she was an 'expert' bringing recalcitrant males to the desired degree of compliance.

Naturally, at her interview, conducted after a few months by Professor Rumple, her marital history was not a subject to be explored so the fact that her four husbands and one lover had fled after a few months of beginning her domestic 're-alignment' programme, remained her secret. It is rumoured that, because of their experiences, the 'graduates' never remarried or took on another female partner. What she did outline at the interview was the basis of her curriculum, which were:

1. Reorganising partners' social events with old pals and determine acceptable ones.

2. Dog walking and cat cuddling.
3. Domestic chores training, including washing and ironing.
4. Cooking for two.
5. Correct bedtime etiquette.
6. How to beat him in an argument. Plus, correct use of force in difficult cases.
7. Ensuring he watches the correct TV programme or listens to acceptable radio programmes.
8. Keeping his mother at bay.
9. Regularly check who he is with and where.

Reorganising social events with old pals

Do not challenge his social diary until week six. Use your female wiles to encourage a reorganised diary. From meeting his pals seven evenings a week, reduce to four, with assurance that he will arrive home in time, to avoid dinner going in the trashcan. If anyone of his so-called friends do not fit your social criteria, they should be banished.

a. If he fails to comply, he sleeps on the sofa. This rule may take a week or two to penetrate his skull.
b. If you ban him seeing certain old 'friends', ensure he doesn't meet them secretly. Engage a female private detective you can rely on. If he's found out disobeying this rule, impose a 28-day sex ban.
c. Once he obeys the four-day-a-week profile, reduce the days one at a time, with the same 'punishment' hanging over him if he strays from the rules.

d. If he fails more than five of the course components in four weeks, deny him sex for five weeks. This will help focus his concentration.

e. If he rebels against these domestic rules, shake a liberal dose of itching powder in all his underpants.

Dog walking and cat cuddling

This is one of the most important part of the re-training programme.

a. It is important he understands the importance of giving your pet Chihuahua its twice a day exercise. It is important he makes friends with your 'lodger', the cat, by combing him/her and feeding and watering the pet on demand.

b. It is important you ensure the dog/cat/rat or other type of pet are kept happy

If he fails to comply then he should be confined to sleeping in the spare bedroom. If he obeys, allow him back to the marital bed at your convenience (see below).

Domestic chores training, including washing and ironing

If you want a trouble-free life with doing as little as possible, the following methods are suggested.

a. Vacuum cleaning and dusting. These are important chores and training should be begun as soon as possible. Make sure he knows the working end of the hose, which spray can is the polish and what a duster looks like. Make sure he is aware that fly killer is not a suitable substitute for spray polish.

This may take some time. Persevere. He'll get the message, eventually.

If he proves to be difficult to train, impose the following rules. Insist he uses the vacuum cleaner until he gets it right. If he proves difficult, apply the following reminders.

1. Lock him in the cupboard with the vacuum cleaner, holding the spray polish and duster. Release when he promises to get it right.
2. If after a few days, he goes back to his old inefficient ways, tell him he sleeps on his own until he gets it right. Also threaten him with denial of his once a week, one-hour meeting with his drunken pals. He'll eventually see the right path.
3. If he regresses, deny him sex all week. Be aware, that after a time without he'll look elsewhere, deny him access to his credit/debit cards so he can't pay for a 'hooker'.

Be aware that after a time without you-know-what he'll look elsewhere. It's in their nature. If you can locate a supply, the good old-fashioned remedy of a spoonful of bromide in their tea will work wonders in reducing their libido.

In my view they must be taught to use the washing machine. I believe it is bad form for his underwear to contaminate your silk knickers and bras.

It is most important he is taught how to use the iron as early as possible, to deal with his own shirts and the correct way to put a crease in trousers. My advice is to get him into this routine before you add your own ironing needs to his tasks. If he starts complaining, or deliberately doing it wrong, hit him with the ultimate sanction or re-introduce a daily dose of bromide and sleeping on his own.

It is important he clearly understands the need to put the rubbish out at the right time on the correct day. He will soon get this right when he is forced to take the black bags to the tip himself and pay for them to be disposed.

Cooking for two
This, in theory, should be easy.

1. He needs to be weaned from reliance on take-aways, particularly from Burger Bars.
2. If he was cooking for himself, he needs to understand that cooking for two merely means doubling the ingredients.
3. If he is unable to get a grip of cooking, send him on a Delia Smith style course.

He needs to understand cooking is an important part of the partnership. Failure to acknowledge this means denial of sleeping rights with you until he improves.

Correct bedtime etiquette
He must learn, within two days of marriage, that, if the aforementioned pet is already ensconced in the marital bed, the pet comes first. If he challenges this, ensure he understands that a total embargo on sex will be enforced for the next seven days.

How to win an argument

Simple. If he won't agree to your point of view, retire to the bedroom and lock the door.

Schedule for watching TV or listening to the radio.

1. Only TV programmes you approve. Carry On films, Dad's Army repeats or cooking programmes are acceptable. Others will be given severe scrutiny. This includes which football, rugby or cricket snooker and darts matches are permissible to watch with your permission.

2. No Radio 4 Today programme, on days John Humphreys is the presenter on the grounds his political stance isn't clearly defined. And he's too tough on nice people.

3. Watching or listening to any programmes will need a 'consent' certificate. In the case of exceptionally good adherence to the rules, a certificate may occasionally be dispensed with. If he fails to comply by hiding a TV or radio in the garden shed, record this as blatant disobedience. Impose the ultimate punishment: no sex for an indefinite period. It is hoped that this will focus his attention on the rules.

The professor read with horror her views and what she was planning as the curriculum. That night he was sitting looking forlornly sat in the snug bar of the *Gripe and Groan* sucking at his unlit briar pipe when the Trio came in for their usual Tuesday night tipple.

The Professor was pondering his own design for courses for men.

He handed the colonel the typewritten sheets.

He read it and laughed. Lenny scanned it and said, "Don't understan' this." Jock scanned it, shook his head, said nothing and handed it back the professor.

The professor sucked the stem of the pipe, which was never alight, and told the Trio he would have to expand the number of courses at the University. "Somehow, I've got to combat the growing success of the worthy success. I would have to design a course for men."

None of the Trio understood what he was talking about. The colonel said later that he had a premonition of problems ahead.

Chapter 8

TWO days later, with the residents protest still in full cry the colonel travelled to a studio facility in South London to meet the producer and director of the planned television drama about bank robbers, *The World of Robbers*. His publishers, Ace & Masters, had organised the meeting. Little did he realise, his story line and theirs would conflict. Initially, he was delighted to be offered a part and receive a credit and payment for being the source of stories. The story line was based, in the main, on his talks and the contents of his proposed book.

He was surprised to discover the two executives were both female.

Marjorie Temple had been a producer of television dramas for some 20 years. She had a no-nonsense approach and spent money freely on the basis that it wasn't coming from her purse. She usually worked on projects with Sarah Smart, a tall, equally no-nonsense director who demanded perfection. She held the record of demanding the most takes for one scene, causing questions to be raised in Parliament about absurd spending by the BBC. Her normal riposte was to wave her hand and say, "If you want the best, you pay the price."

Marjorie did a brisk introduction and asked the colonel for a brief summary of his life of crime.

The colonel told them that robbing banks, post offices and security vans had been exciting when he was young, but it then developed into a business that wasn't always profitable and usually led to time ensconced in one of Her Majesty's 'holiday homes', run by the Prison Service.

Sarah leaned forward holding her glass of Chablis and said, "Darling, we have to make this exciting, lots of action, you know, car chases and all that."

The colonel went to add something and was silenced.

"Now, just be quiet whilst I plan the scene, yes, yes, I've got it, you let off the gun, grab the money and run out of the bank and into a waiting car and speed away, followed by a police car with its blue flashing lights and siren sounding. A high-speed chase."

The colonel attempted to interrupt and was silenced. "It didn't usually 'appen like that, yer see…"

"Now do be quiet, colonel, we have to make this exciting for the viewer."

Marjorie interrupted, "Don't let facts spoil a good story."

The colonel again tried to explain and was told to shut up.

"We can use your story lines, suitably embellished, to excite the viewer."

The colonel gave then a disapproving look and stood up. "Your so-called embellished facts will spoil the truth. Our bank robberies didn't involve high-speed chases. We didn't always blow a hole in the ceilin', grab the cash and run. Just sound work by good cops got us nicked, you're just a load of fantasists, bending the truth fer the sake of ratings. You disgust me. I don't want anything to do wiv this programme."

The colonel limped out, waving his walking stick, leaving two astonished looking TV executives staring after him.

Late that afternoon, over a pint, he told local police Sergeant Wallace off duty at the *Gripe and Groan* about his meeting with the two women television executives. "Barmy they were, damn barmy. They believed every robbery involved guns going off and high-speed chases. God, what idiots. Didn't even tell me what I could earn for helping them."

"Well, that's the world of television for yer," Wallace replied as he stood up, holding two empty pint glasses and headed for the bar and a re-fill.

Meanwhile, back in South London the two TV executives were not going to have their lucrative series ruined by a throwback old-time bank robber who didn't like their ideas. With some help from a couple of dubious crime reporters and young researchers, they set about rescuing their project.

As the colonel and Wallace chatted, in a country pub near Bogwash members of SOBS were meeting after they had heard that Miss Creswell was still offering special spanking services. There were a number of them with black eyes and swollen lips, none would say how the injuries occurred. One of the unscarred women produced a copy of The Bugle showing an advert declaring Creswell was back in business. It also carried a story of the demonstration showing her placard.

Clive 'Cracker' Crumb was called to a meeting at one of the 'offices' believing he was going to get hired to 'sort someone out'. There was no mention of an all-female fight in a Brighton pub. They'd discovered he'd lied about his meeting with Miss Creswell and frightening her away. She had, in fact, left on holiday before he had arrived at her flat.

One of the ladies looked at him sweetly, as he began unbuckling his trouser belt. He thought he'd been forgiven for his mistake and was going to enjoy the next few minutes. WRONG.

A second lady picked-up a large jug of water with many ice cubes.

Crackers rapidly rising, feelings of desire were suddenly extinguished when the cold water was poured over his exposed nether region. He was told his contract had ended and he wouldn't receive his usual cash and kind rewards.

One of the 'ladies' said they really ought to visit Creswell and persuade her to join their group and earn bigger fees.

Meanwhile, quietly at home, Joanna was beginning to reflect the teaching of the English language was not as good as it was when she was a headmistress teaching the subject. The number of her male students needing mild chastising and severe punishment, was growing. It confirmed something that she had believed for a long time; men were more stupid than women.

She kept a variety of styles and weights of cane. Some used on the palm of the miscreant's hand or others used on their bare buttocks. She never ceased to be amazed at the number of well spoken, smartly dressed men, apparently professionals, who opted for the bare, rear-end application. Their numbers were increasing daily.

Chapter 9

AS the colonel struggled to understand the television company's latest outline script and Jock and Lenny went about their routine tasks for the Tartanettes, a series of armed robberies were occurring in the Home Counties, all involving four elderly men. Police investigating the outbreak quickly realised the blagging had all the hallmarks of the old Gang of Four. Several raids had occurred before Met detectives located that the colonel and his 'crew' were living in a residential home in Bogwash. Without travelling to Bogwash, the Met boys were able to substantiate alibis by talking to Sergeant Wallace and—at his suggestion—the retired judge in their last trial.

As the enquiry was underway, Detective Inspector Bernard 'Bernie' Bamber was investigating a Croydon, south London bank robbery carried out that morning by four oldies. Only back on duty after six months' suspension following a messed-up investigation, he believed he was the best detective in the Metropolitan police. His critics said he was unable to solve a blatant case of shoplifting. Some colleagues claimed he'd never actually solved a single crime and had earned promotion by developing the skills of making sure it was 'Buggins turn'. He was Buggins.

Some years before, he had made-up the numbers when a raid captured the notorious Gang of Four. He was now sure he had the answer to the present gang. He failed to read any intelligence reports regarding other bank robberies with similar characteristics involving four old men, known as the Gang of Four, who had been absolved of any responsibility for the current spate of heists. The same report also mentioned that one of the four had died some months before.

Bamber had developed the unshakeable belief the remaining three of the original gang were presently residing in Bogwash. Without telling his Met bosses or anyone senior officer in Bogwash, he headed for the seaside town in a marked squad car along with four junior officers in a van to arrest the gang. He didn't want the locals or any other forces having the pleasure of such a nick. It was to be his way back into favour with his superiors.

It was around noon when Bamber and his team pulled up noisily outside the Retreat, yelled "Police" into the intercom, ignored Stella Stern's "Can I help you?" marched into the ground floor lounge where the colonel, Jock and Lenny had just assembled for the midday stroll to the *Gripe and Groan* and arrested them on suspicion of armed robbery.

Their protests of innocence and telling Bamber they had buried Reg some months before, were ignored, and they were taken to Croydon nick and incarcerated in the cells. Bamber laid on his bullying style of interrogation technique and told all three they would remain in custody until they disclosed where Reg was hiding.

"Where's he hiding? Make it easy on yerself and confess," Bamber bellowed at the colonel, accusing him of masterminding the raids and demanding to know the whereabouts of Reg Crowley, who he accused of hiding out with the sole aim of confusing his investigations.

Bamber produced a strange kind of noise: half cough, half sort of chuckle.

To regain his composure and audible speech, he gestured to his sergeant to keep the three under surveillance and left the interview room. After an undignified coughing bout in the corridor which the two colleagues left there on duty, guarding the door, pretended not to notice, he told them proudly he'd 'got the gang' and nearly had a fatal return of his cough when one of his subordinates suggested very mildly that he might be barking up the wrong tree.

When Scotland Yard chiefs were told what Bamber had done, the local commander was ordered to, 'Sort this out', and he decided to take his frustration out on a golf ball at some nearby links, his obsessional beliefs.

The Trio, colonel, Jock and Lenny, decided Bamber could provide a lot more entertainment than a ball and clubs. As one, they stated categorically, they could show him Reg's hiding place.

An hour and a half later, following a high-speed return to Bogwash, they stood in the churchyard at St Jaspers, opposite the Retreat, and showed Bamber Reg's gravestone. He demanded they produce evidence of the internment. Police records gave details of the robberies, the old Gang of Four were said to have carried out. The vicar happily obliged with details of the funeral and the colonel provided details of where he was giving talks to members of the legal profession.

The colonel suggested Bamber had Reg's dig up coffin just to prove it was Lenny's corpse. "You could always get DNA samples just to seal the fact it's Lenny," he calmly told the hyperactive detective, who hardly contain his desire to knock the three out cold.

All the girls of the Tartanettes and the Guy and Gorilla band vouched that Lenny had driven the ladies to the Pavilion for rehearsals and Jock played his bagpipes. Retired High Court, Judge Guy Carrington-Worth confirmed he saw Jock and Lenny at the event whilst he and the band, Guy and the Gorillas, were practicing.

As the three were being reluctantly released, Bamber warned them, "I'm watching you lot and I'll get yer in the end." He then returned to the comfort of Croydon nick. While the Trio were being released from custody a Luton bank had been raided by four 'old men'.

The Bogwash police force, on learning of this incident, had their best laugh of the week at Bamber's expense. But the new, Assistant Chief Constable, William Watkins, complained to the Met. Commander Martin Freeman, who groaned when told who was behind Bogwash debacle. He was no fan of Bamber. He headed for the whisky bottle when told that Bamber refused to believe Reg Crowther had died during the other three's trial.

Sitting in the squad room at Croydon nick, Inspector Bamber was still repeating to anyone who would listen that a retired judge, a room full of lawyers, bankers and a group of old ladies masquerading as a group of Burlesque dancers had been bribed to give false alibis.

The colonel, Lenny and Jock vowed they would find the identity of the real gang. "How dare they copy my methods," the colonel growled as he waved his walking stick around. It would take some weeks to establish who the 'copy cats' were.

In a back-street house in an Oxford semi-detached, four men met up, then headed for their heist of the Four Counties bank in Hounslow, unaware the Trio had just been arrested, questioned and released from custody in Bogwash. A stolen Mark 2 Jaguar awaited them in a lock-up garage on a nearby housing estate.

Later that evening, Detective Inspector Bamber stared incredulously at his computer screen as he read the report on the Hounslow blagging in which four old men, one driving the getaway car, had carried out. Three cups of coffee and two fags later, he announced to an empty office, "Two gangs masterminded by the bloody colonel."

He began to believe there were two gangs under the leadership of the colonel. "Yes, that was the answer," he muttered to himself.

Meanwhile, the colonel was contacting old friends in London's underworld to establish who were the four old men using his techniques on banks and post offices? He drew a blank. As did Jock and Lenny, as they tried old contacts with no results. The identity of the four remained a mystery.

The next day, the top-brass at Scotland Yard summoned Bamber to a meeting and warned him that he had upset some top-people, and his allegations against the Bogwash three didn't stand-up as they had impeachable alibis. They ordered him to concentrate on other matters. That afternoon, he convinced an overworked police doctor that he was suffering from stress and needed to rest. He was to put on sick leave and immediately headed for his mother's quiet country cottage near Salisbury. He was becoming increasingly sure top brass were protecting the four villains. Four, because there was no way Reg Crowther could be dead.

As he headed for his mother's Wiltshire home, squads of riot police were deployed to contain fighting in a back-street Brighton pub. A group of women, young and old, were being ejected after a fight broke out and three women needed hospital treatment, along with four men, who tried to quell the fighting only to be left howling in pain and holding their private parts. Police dogs barked loudly but refused their handlers' commands to tackle the fighting women.

The incident petered out as most of the women gradually fell and passed out, mainly due to a surfeit of alcohol. Injured men beat a hasty retreat. The police could not establish what lay behind the conflict. Two women, garishly dressed, appeared before magistrates the next morning, and they were each fined £100 with costs for public order offences.

When the reasons for the fighting were discovered, it caused high-level discussions among senior police. They had difficulty deciding which of them would question a High Court Judge and a Chief Constable who shared their predilection among the operatives of SOBS who were fighting over 'First Spanking Rights'.

At the Gripe and Groan, there were two distinctive educational groups, Professor Rumple and his male domination courses and at the opposite side of the bats are Celia Worthy and her 'Females Should Be The Boss' campaign. The local gay community sided with her ideas.

It was clear there was animosity between the professor and Celia.

The landlord warned them to keep the loud critical shouts from either side to a whisper. Celia took this as a male-dominated threat. She and her group were barred for a week.

Chapter 10

INTELLECTUAL ability is alien to Lenny and had been recognised by the education system, police, probation service and the prison system for some years. Those who knew him well recognised his strange belief that TV and film stars were 'moonlighting', in a variety of roles, whilst resting. His latest idea was that carers and council workers in Bogwash belonged to this group of actors and were regularly seen at the Retreat or in local pubs.

Sergeant Wallace had joined the colonel and Jock at the *Gripe and Groan*. Lenny was driving six members of the Tartanettes to a music shop in Brighton.

Jock suddenly asked, "Who's this Lumsden woman he thinks that woman Belinda really is?"

"Not a clue," the colonel replied. "Just another one of his fantasy trips."

"Happens a lot, does it?" Wallace asked.

"Too true, had to get him outa many a pickle because he thinks some stranger is a TV actor or film star," the colonel responded.

Jock sipped his whisky, then quietly asked the colonel, Remember that episode in a South London pub? He was convinced a man standing at the bar was Sean Connery.

"What 'appened?" Wallace asked.

"We had learned the hard way not to challenge his ideas, we knew from bitter experience he would throw a tantrum with anyone saying he was wrong," Jock replied in an intelligible form of English, with a Scot's accent.

The colonel continued, "I remember an episode that these beliefs almost got him arrested, following an incident in a South London pub, it would have, potentially, been his only sentence not connected to armed robbery if the man involved had pressed charges.

"This happened whilst Reg was still alive. The four of us were celebrating our release from Long Lartin after serving four years, from one of our 'holiday periods' courtesy of the prison service.

"Lenny had already downed three pints of Fuller's Best Bitter when he spotted someone at the bar he was convinced was Sean Connery, 'slumming it'. This was soon after the release of the Bond film, *Never Say Never Again.*

"Lenny decided he wanted the man's autograph. Despite efforts to stop him, he staggered over to the man standing alone at the bar. He was dressed in mud-stained trousers, a grubby looking cheque shirt, a donkey jacket and wore muddy boots. A clever disguise, Lenny had decided.

"He had a note book in his hand and a ballpoint pen; he approached the man and asked, 'Scuse me Sean, can I have yer autograph?'

"The man was in the process of taking a gulp from his pint of Guinness. After he'd taken a gulp, he wiped the froth from his lips with the back of his hand and asked. 'Wotcha want? His language was unmistakeably West of Ireland.

"'Your autograph.'

"'Bog off, yer pratt,' the man said as he took another gulp of Guinness.

"'C'mon Sean,' he said, 'I know it's you, hiding from yer public. What about yer signature? He thrust the notebook and pen at the man.'

"Jock interrupted, it was comical really. Slowly the man said, 'Me names Liam, 'ave yer got that, yer brainless idiot.' He knocked the notebook and pen from Lenny's outstretched hand. With one hand, the Irishman grabbed Lenny's chin and growled, 'Listen pillock brain, me name isn't Sean, it's Liam, got it.' He pushed Lenny away and added, 'Now bog off.'"

The colonel continued, "Lenny bent down and picked up his notebook and pen, and as he rose up, he gave Liam a hefty clout on the side of the head. Before the Irishman could retaliate, Lenny threw the remains of the man's drink over him.

"We managed to get to him and drag him away. The landlord managed to stop the Irishman as we shoved Lenny outa the door, just as the cops arrived."

Jock took up the story, "What 'appened next wuz straight oota a comedy. It really wuz."

The colonel continued, "Two cops went inta the pub and two stayed with Lenny and the next thing we know is the return of one of the two cops that went inside. He told us the Irishman wouldn't press charges if the autograph hunter bought him a Guinness and he was thrilled that Lenny thought he was a film star and that was the end of the matter. I went in and bought him a pint of Guinness."

"Ye wouldn't believe the number of times we had to rescue him for his idea someone was famous. Say no more. Lenny's just arrived."

Chapter 11

THE colonel was beginning to enjoy writing his memories of his time as a full-time robber and telling about others in the same trade. His talks were becoming popular with the legal profession. Visiting Cambridge, he was to give his first talk on the activities of others in the same business, whom he had met over the years.

"When I first began writing my life story I thought me and me team held the record as the most incompetent. On researchin', I soon discovered we had competition."

There was a ripple of laughter.

"I wuz chattin' to an old cop pal, I'd gotten to know him after he nicked us a couple of times. He told me of a member of one gang who announced what he and his pals were plannin'."

"They'd nicked a Ford Zephyr that had parked outside the bank in Basildon, Essex. Three of them ran in, all tooled-up wearin' boiler suits and their faces covered by masks. Outside, the driver of the Ford was invited to leave the comfort of the car by four uniformed officers.

"A little later his three pals were led in handcuffs and missing their masks from the bank by armed officers. You

71

may think a case of the wrong place at the wrong time. Not quite.

"One of those arrested was eighteen-years-old and reeked of alcohol. It came as a surprise to him that the man he had befriended in a Romford pub was tall, with a broken nose and a cauliflower ear, was an off-duty Armed Robbery Squad sergeant and a member of the Yard's amateur boxing team. The youngster believed the battered looking forty-year-old was an East End villain and as he downed a couple more pints, he boasted to the officer what he and his pals were plannin' for later that day. He couldn't keep his mouth shut. Both Met and Essex teams awaited the gang's appearance.

"It turned out it was their first attempt at a blaggin'. The oldest was twenty-two. They all got weighed off at Chelmsford for ten years each.

"I understand it was the last time they attempted to join the big time."

The audience clapped and laughed.

The colonel warmed to the audience reaction.

"Let me tell you of a robbery that even caused us professionals great amusement. This incident happened at a small post office near Harlow. The blaggin' was carried out by a single robber whose getaway transport was a high-powered motorcycle. Soon after, an ambulance and a local police car attended an accident on a road leading to the M11. The bag lying nearby was discovered to contain eight-thousand smackers. It was soon realised, the robbery and the injured rider were connected.

"On removin' the rider's crash helmet, paramedics and police were surprised to discover a forty-five-year-old blonde. It turned out, her boyfriend and others had been sent down some months before for armed robbery. She had lost her breadwinner and had decided to take-over some robberies he was plannin'. She hadn't accounted fer a deer leepin' out of a hedge and she swerved to avoid it and crashed her bike. She was sent down for twelve years.

"She served five years and some years later, I came across Florence Foster again. She'd paid the fees to join our trainin' school. She wanted to be a better blagger.

"Let me tell you of a bank robbery that went wrong with the vanishing getaway car. I learned about this tale when banged-up in Leicester jail. Bradford in Yorkshire was well out of our operating area. The two bloggers involved in this saga were from a Manchester mob. They told me how they got caught. It seems they'd nicked a top of the range Mercedes, put false number plates on it and parked it, unlocked and the keys in the ignition, outside the bank as part of a quick getaway. The two of them ran in all tooled-up, wearing sunglasses. Just remember this was before the days of wall-to-wall CCTV.

"They persuaded the teller to hand over the cash in the till then fled out the front door to find their getaway car had gone. The two ran to a nearby bus stop and caught the number 17. There were no other passengers.

"The two were caught at a police road block and the money recovered. They were annoyed that someone had stolen the car they had stolen.

"It seems another gang looking for a suitable getaway vehicle had spotted the Merc outside the bank, unlocked and with the keys in the ignition. Two days later, it was used in the getaway from a raid on a post office in Salford. It was on a new set of moody number plates.

"When I was told about this, I discovered the matter didn't end there, it transpired, it lay behind a jail riot. The two gangs found themselves sharing the same wing in a Midlands jail and the two that had originally stolen the Merc discovered how the second gang had nicked it and used it on their own blaggin.

"The two collared the leader of the second gang and gave him a painful reminder they were 'top dogs'. Whilst their leader lay in the hospital wing his three pals sought out the duo who had beaten their boss. Both had to be treated in an outside hospital with life threatening injuries.

"The undercover communication network went into overdrive and fighting broke out between supporters of both gangs. The prison authorities declared a riot. There were many injuries and prisoners were transferred to other jails.

"When both gangs were finally released from choky, they established a hate campaign against each other. Each blaming the other for any armed robberies in the North.

"As I said, we were stupid, but we were intelligent in comparison with these lunatics. They really hated each other and spent more time dreaming up plans to have the opposition shopped for any robbery even when they could provide a good alibi. They spent so much energy in shopping each other they ran out of money and credibility even with their own community.

"In our most inept times, we couldn't match their stupidity.

"Both groups were eventually charged with threatening behaviour and wasting police time; they were warned about their future conduct. I was told both sides were very embarrassed as it was the first time they'd appeared in court and not been jailed.

"I laughed at the final indignity when the gang leader of the four hoods discovered that the daughter he idolised had become pregnant, by one of the two oppositions blaggers. As I've said many times, you can't always legislate for the absurd."

The audience clapped and laughed.

Chapter 12

AN ANNOYED suspended policeman Bamber settled into his old childhood bedroom determined to prove entirely of his own bat, the aged Gang of Four were behind the robberies. He would assess the 'evidence' over a meal and a pint in a Salisbury pub.

At around the same time, the colonel was giving a talk to a group of retired judges, barristers and solicitors in the Inner Temple. He began, "The story I'm going to tell dates from the late sixties. I'd carefully planned to rob a bank in Croydon which I knew was about to receive a large sum to cover the week's wages for several local businesses.

"One of my team acquired a red Jaguar saloon, well we nicked it." The audience chuckled. "Our favourite type of getaway vehicle. I'd planned the raid down to finest detail; how many guards, the exact time and the best getaway route. Now, at that time in South London, we were the best-known armed robbery gang. It was just bits of bad luck that got us caught."

A QC piped up, "I defended you, and you all still got ten years."

The colonel coughed and continued, "We covered our faces by pulling down the balaclavas, checked the sawn-off shotguns were loaded and jumped out of the car and ran towards the bank. That's when things went wrong, three other men identically dressed, appeared from the opposite direction and confronted us at the front door.

"Now, ladies and gentlemen, there were two-armed robbery teams trying to rob the same bank. Behind the camouflage of his woollen mask, I recognised the unmistakeable lisp of East End fellow blagger, Victor, The Voice, Vicente. A hard man, if ever there was. He led a gang that made the Kray twins look like pacifists. A mixture of laughing and a shout of "Oh, yeah" came from the audience.

Not to be put off, the colonel continued, "He shoved his gun in my direction and threatened he'd blow us away if we didn't get out of his way. We stood our ground and after a few choice words, a fight broke out and we were slinging punches in the street outside the bank and things were getting nasty until about a dozen armed cops had arrived along two ambulances drew up plus two fire engines. A standoff between us, Vicente's mob and the cops, which was only solved when the police encouraged both fire engines to turn their hoses on us. Vincente and one of his henchmen were driven some 15 feet along the pavement and ended up in hospital. Neither m'self or me three colleagues were hurt. Just wet. I've never understood why Vincente didn't use his sawn-offs on us. It turned out they weren't loaded. I later learned, he couldn't afford the advance fees to his gunsmith for the cartridges as well as the guns.

"The cops nicked us all and we spent three years in choky for affray, attempted armed robbery and having no licence for the sawn-off shotguns. Vincente and his henchmen got a further ten years for the robbery of a security van they' done two months earlier in Twickenham. We laughed when we discovered it wasn't carrying cash. We understood the embarrassment.

"The most embarrasin' thing fer me and me plannin' was that the bank had closed the previous day followin' a merger. It turned out that Vincente had retired one of his henchmen for plannin' stupidity. No one saw him again."

The audience of legal minds chuckled and applauded at his anecdote. He went on, "Many of the public at large have a strange view of the robbery business. For instance, a couple of weeks ago I was invited to a meeting with two lady television executives who wanted to create a programme on me and me team's activities.

"I soon realised that these two had little or no idea what robbin' banks or post offices was all about. They thought we swanned in, guns blazing, blowin' people away and destroyin' a perfectly good ceilin'. This they'd partially got right, killin' people weren't our style. The girlfriend of one blagger convinced them our getaways was very excitin' and involved high-speed car chases. All fiction, as I know you ladies and gents are aware. These scenarios didn't exist, they were fiction. We never blew people away, in fact, we were proud that no one ever got hurt from our activities. I openly admit, we caused many good ceilings to be replaced.

"As fer high-speed car chases with us firin' at police. Never 'appened. As I told these two wimmin. We only got caught because we were known as the busiest blaggers in the business and good detective work got our collars felt. Simple as that.

"Their plans were just fiction masquerading as fact, just to get high ratings. They weren't interested in the truth. I made it clear, I wasn't interested in fiction all I want is an honest tale about how useless we were at armed robbery."

The audience clapped enthusiastically.

However, the efforts to create the TV programme unleashed a crime solving solution least expected. Other gangs, including Vincente, were delighted to receive the largesse offered by the TV company in return for telling of their best robberies. As part of the programme, senior police officers were invited to see the unedited 'rushes' and make comments.

Detectives watching the pre-release programme laughed to bursting point when they heard Vincente's and others contribution. Suddenly, they had on-screen confessions of the culprits to many unsolved blaggin's. The only 'mob' not mentioned or interviewed were the old Gang of Four, now the Trio.

Within hours of the first episodes airing, police raided addresses in London, the Home counties, the Midlands, Manchester and Glasgow had arrested more than sixty, self-confessed, bank, post office and security van robbers all basking in the glare of publicity, as they recounted their finest hours to the petite, good looking blonde interviewer.

The colonel, Lenny and Jock heard the news through the grapevine and then the media. They cheered with glee. The colonel was glad he'd turned down the offer to appear in the documentary. They slapped themselves on the back for having the nous in refusing to appear on the programme.

In his countryside hideaway, Bernie Bamber watched the programme on the night right the way through to the last syllable of the credits, at which point, he literally began to tear his hair out muttering, "Where the 'ell are those four villains?" He was infuriated that the arrest list didn't include the Gang of Four and they hadn't appeared in the programme. He still wouldn't believe that Reg Crowther was dead. He muttered, "Where are they hiding him and why? I've gotta find out."

Some months later, Vincente claimed at his trial he was a misunderstood Sicilian immigrant and he'd come to England to get away from the Mafia influence and he was really a law-abiding citizen and the police hounded him because of his family background.

The prosecution pointed out that he'd been born in a Southend hospital and his grandparents had come to England in the late 1930s to escape the Mussolini regime and his mother was English. He had developed the little fractured Italian speech he had, following an early prison term aged 22, when he shared a cell with an Italian fraudster.

His defence barrister claimed Vincente was misunderstood—a member of the jury was heard to mutter, "Not surprising, the way he talks"—as the barrister added he was a "Good boy and had never hurt anyone." He was sentenced to twenty years. On being dragged from the court, he shouted that the Gang of Four were to blame for this miscarriage of justice and he would get his revenge. Oddly his outburst was expressed in fluent, Essex-boy understandable English.

Chapter 13

AT THE RETREAT the colonel, Lenny and Jock read reports of the trial with amusement and relief. At last the truth was out: they hadn't committed any robberies north of Oxford, in Bristol or anywhere in the west country.

Most of the tenants in the Retreat continued their quiet way of life. Walter Windsor, a long-time retired small-time villain, was about to come better known. He was bored with the style of living at the Retreat. Now, aged ninety-years-old he was about to come, again, to police attention for the most absurd reason. He'd had a colourful criminal past, including being a wartime black marketeer and period as an 'enforcer' for the notorious south London Clarkson gang.

In his seventies, he disappeared off the judicial radar. For some four years, his red Vauxhall Astra had been parked in the small car park at the Retreat. Walter, or 'Wally' to his friends, had had his licence revoked after failing his eyesight test.

He didn't mix with other tenants but was occasionally seen visiting a local convenience store dressed in clothes that hadn't seen a washing machine for some time. His body odour kept fellow-residents at a distance. Shopkeepers left doors open and went around with scented spray after he had visited them. The Trio were lucky that they never come across him in or out of the building.

His only regular visitors were the twice daily and employees of the Bogwash care company, Boggy Care, who had learned to cope with his smell and the disarray of his flat. His lack of concern for personal hygiene was only exceeded by his total disregard for the law which was about to manifest itself.

One wet Wednesday afternoon, he was seen getting into his old Vauxhall which surprisingly started after a couple of attempts. He drove out of the car park in a series of jerky movements and nearly collided with a car going past the entrance.

He'd managed to get to the roundabout leading onto the two-lane by-pass where he was spotted driving the wrong way around it at an estimated speed of five-miles-per hour and narrowly avoiding oncoming traffic. After four attempts he managed to get onto the correct side of the by-pass where he proceeded at a stately ten miles per hour.

Speedy drivers were suddenly reduced to a crawl believing they were in a 'rolling road' orchestrated by the police. Those at the front expressed their frustration with many horns being sounded and head lights rapidly flashing as they crawled behind the Vauxhall which weaved alarmingly between the inner and outer lanes.

A mile away on another roundabout, PC Sarah Simms was told to position her patrol car on the dual carriageway and block and detain the driver of a red Vauxhall. She parked her BMW estate blocking both carriageways with her blue lights flashing and waited for the red car to come around the bend. She ran for cover as she realised it wasn't going to stop.

Wally ploughed into the left side door of the patrol car at an estimated five miles an hour leaving a massive dent in it.

Sarah opened the driver's door of the Vauxhall. Wally was tightly holding the steering wheel muttering, "Where the bloody hell did that come from. Shouldn't be there. Damned dangerous and illegal."

Sarah held a handkerchief to her face to cope with the odour from Wally. Two male colleagues persuaded him to leave the car and tried to encourage him to take a roadside breathalyser and drug test, which he refused, saying he'd had nothing to drink nor took drugs, so why should he. He was arrested.

When Sarah had recovered from the shock, she burst into tears. She had her favourite patrol car back that morning after being repaired following a previous crash involving a stolen car.

Back at Bogwash nick, a check soon discovered Wally had no driving licence and had no insurance or a MOT certificate for the car. His licence had been revoked because of his poor eyesight. He refused to take a breath test on the evidential machine claiming he hadn't been drinking and was driving carefully.

The police surgeon interviewed him leaving them frustrated. Wally thought it was funny that he'd caused so much chaos and had damaged a police car. He argued that he was of an age that put him beyond the law and was driving safely. He claimed this will all police intimidation, even corruption, and the crash wouldn't have happened if a stupid cop hadn't blocked his way. The doctor issued a notice declaring him unfit to plead and he was taken to the psychiatric wing of Bogwash hospital.

No one seemed to miss him at the Retreat, but the absence of the red car was commented on.

A day later, Jock was told to stop practising his bagpipe playing in the rear garden of the Retreat as the noise was upsetting the tenants.

Lenny had an hour's tutorial from Miss Creswell. He wasn't punished for his bad English diction.

Chapter 14

AS the maniac driver saga unfolded involving the Police Complaints Commission, Bamber sat in his country hideaway believing he had been prevented from exposing the real villains, he was sure his Divisional Commander and other Met top brass were corrupt and part of the cover up. Bamber planned the next part of his exposure.

Elsewhere, Jock had found, what he believed, was the perfect location for practicing his bagpipe playing. It was on the edge of a wood, some two miles from the nearest dwelling. This day, he was going through his repertoire when suddenly he looked-up and saw a herd of some thirty brown and white cows looking over the fence at him, all with their right leg raised, they were swishing their tails and swaying their heads in synchrony with his interpretation of the tune, *Scotland, the Brave.*

Every day, for another week, he went to the same spot and played a variety of highland tunes on his pipes and occasionally used his piano accordion. He was soon surrounded by the audience, of brown and white cows. They seemed to be intently appreciating his repertoire. He was amused by his new fan club.

On the afternoon of the seventh day of his practice sessions, a man on a four-wheeled quad bike stopped in the field alongside the cows and shouted, "So, it be you, these cows seem infatuated wiv and the bloody noise. I should thank yer, they're milk yield 'as bin the best, ever. Seems they like the noise, anyway where are yer from?"

"I live in the toon."

"I mean, you're obviously a Scot, where from?"

I was born in Perth, but lived most of me life in Glasgee, now here."

The farmer looked puzzled, then said, "D'you mean Glasgow?"

"Ay, that's what I said. I now live in Bogwash." He took a swig of whisky from a half-bottle he kept in his jacket pocket then began blowing air into the bag of his pipes ready to continue his rendition of some obscure Scottish airs.

The farmer shouted, well, you just keep playin', me cows like the noise, it keeps 'em 'appy'. The farmer gave a thumbs-up and rode slowly away, calling for his cows to follow. It was milking time. The herd dutiful followed the quad bike and the calling farmer.

For six days, it rained heavily, preventing Jock practicing in the wood. On the seventh day, he was told someone was at the reception area of the Retreat and wanted to talk to him. It was the farmer.

"I finally found yer, it's about me cows, any chance yer can come back and play them pipe things?"

"Bagpipes," Jock responded.

"Yeah, them things. It's just that their milk yield 'as dropped since you stopped playin'. Any chance yer can start again, I'll pay yer a little summit."

"Sounds weird t'me, a coo giving more milk 'cos of me pipes," Jock responded. "What sort of coos are they?"

"Cows, yer mean?"

"Ay, that's what I said."

"They be Ayrshires, yeah Ayrshires."

Jock took another swig of whisky and smiled, "That explains it, then. Good Scottish coos. They appreciate good highland music and respect the sound of the pipes."

The dairy farmer added, "I need to move the herd to fresh pastures in a couple of days. It's the next-door field. You'll visit 'em, will yer?"

"Fer sure," Jock answered.

For the next ten days, Jock played his pipes to the herd with good results. The farmer rewarded him well. Then Jock hit on an idea. The cows took to the scheme and surrounded the loudspeaker connected to a battery powered CD-player. Jock had found some old disks of Scottish pipe bands.

The piped music had the same effect as Jock's solo live pipe playing. He even found some long-forgotten recordings of Jimmy Stewart from the 1960s. 'The wee fella' who was the star of the old TV programme, *The White Heather Club.* The cows seemed to enjoy his singing. The milk yield rose.

The *Farmers Weekly* magazine reported on the bagpipe and accordion loving cows. Owners of herds of Jersey, Friesian and Holstein milking herds tried this new form of 'in the field' cattle entertainment, they all reported lower milk yields as their herds ran away from the noise. Only Ayrshire milking herds using this form of bovine entertainment increased their daily pint production. Playing music in the milking parlour was not new. Alfresco music, particularly Scottish, was.

With his agricultural escapade on hold, Jock spent more time at rehearsals with the Tartanettes. They were beginning to get new bookings. Thankfully for him, Martha was on holiday in France and wasn't due back for a month. Jock was experiencing peace from her exuberance and her declaration of love for him. He wouldn't admit he was missing her attention.

Chapter 15

TWO weeks had elapsed, and three more post office raids were pulled off by the mystery gang. Jock was visiting his daughter in Edinburgh. Lenny was struggling to improve his English at one of Joanna's lessons whilst the colonel walked along the bank of the river Boggy dreaming up another series of his memories of his criminal past. He joined Sergeant Wallace and a rookie constable to enjoy a pint whilst one of the robberies was taking place.

The Crown Prosecution Service decided that Wally Windsor was un-fit to stand trial. He was detained under The Mental Health Act and confined to a secure hospital. The council acted quickly by fumigating his flat, re-decorating and replacing the carpets.

From his mother's home, Bamber told his police bosses, "He was too ill to do anything." He remained convinced Reg Crowther was alive and well and being hidden by the other three. He couldn't explain why this was happening and was increasingly sure they were being protected by a group of top judges, lawyers, police top brass and wealthy businessmen, all secret members of the gang. His growing belief was they funded the gang's activities and took a large cut of the proceeds. He was going to expose the scandal.

On his first day back, at Croydon, from his sick leave, he tried to persuade sceptical senior officers that the gang had filled the coffin with bricks and pretended it was Reg Crowther. Police top brass were unaware of his plan to dig up the Reg's grave to prove the coffin was full of bricks. His theory was ridiculed. Bamber was delighted when the coffin was exhumed, and the remains of Reg's body were found in the coffin. DNA proved it, but no bricks. He went back into hiding at his boyhood home. His mother didn't ask why he was back, at least he could paint the garden shed and take his anger out on logs he chopped up for the open fire in the cottage.

It was discovered what he had done and was ordered back to Croydon, he was suspended from duty and had his warrant card taken from him pending an investigation. He had forged signatures and issued false exhumation documentation. Police colleagues were delighted with his absence, they could now get on with sensible policing.

From his country retreat, at his mother's Wiltshire home, he began assembling what he believed was evidence against the Gang of Four. He refused to acknowledge Reg was dead. He became reclusive and began to believe any bit of tittle-tattle in the media supported his theory. He was increasingly convinced high-powered people were backing the robberies and were giving the gang false alibis for carrying out the blagging. He was determined to prove his bizarre theory that police top brass, judges and lawyers were part of a well-organised corrupt organisation. The Police Complaints Commission were in no hurry to investigate the allegations that senior officers were behind the raids or deal with his suspension when they heard of his 'fanciful' claims.

The double bass player with Guy and the Gorillas, Sir George Carter, a former solicitor and a now retired member of parliament, was dissuaded from asking a still serving former political colleague from raising a question in The House about a suspended policeman accusing judges and other luminaries of being in the pay of a gang of bank robbers. He was advised it could open 'a whole can of worms' and the press would jump on the allegations with glee. All was quiet, for now.

Back in Bogwash, Lenny and Jock supported the Tartanettes efforts to be top performers with their high-kicking stage act, backed by the musical talents of Guy and the Gorillas, plus Jocks bagpipe playing, dressed in his kilt and other highland regalia.

Lenny worked hard on improving his English, the lessons did little for his intellectual improvement. One strange aspect of his time with Joanna was the lack of punishment for him when he got things wrong.

The colonel walked along the riverside footpath dreaming up more of the historical escapades of 'The Trio's' failure as a successful gang of robbers and the odd-ball characters he'd met whilst 'banged-up', for his failed attempts to become wealthy.

Henry Style continued to try and sell his latest 'superb' investment scheme to elderly lady tenants of the Retreat, there were no takers. Belinda Bennett had advised fellow tenants and landlords against his 'dead cert winner'.

Joanna was being more careful about clients and was only canning those she thought were well educated and were deliberately being naughty. Lenny enjoyed the lessons and escaped punishment even when he got it wrong.

Chapter 16

THE outbreak of bank raids by, apparently, four old men were baffling to the police and 'The Trio's' alibis were rock solid. The raids were also bothering members of the Southern Division of the National Bank Robbers Federation. Those carrying out the raids weren't registered with them. The secretary of the NBRF, Thomas 'Tommy' Gunn, made it clear to police contacts that his members were not responsible.

Members were becoming restless and demanded action to stop the blaggers who were freelancing and taking their business away from them. An extraordinary general meeting was called, the colonel, Lenny and Jock were invited, even though they were no longer active members.

Tommy Gunn called the meeting at a large central London hotel. 267 members along with the Trio turned up. Tommy stood on a footstool and opened the meeting. "Gentlemen," a female voice sitting near the front shouted, "and ladies."

He responded to the 'lady' sitting with two others and replied, "and them too." He cleared his throat with a short cough and carried on. "Now, we've come 'ere today to discuss an outbreak of robberies that's nowt to do wiv our members. Me, other committee members, and our security team 'ave carried out a thorough investigation and proven none of our members 'ave been involved.

"Seven, who we thought could be involved are now bein' looked after in a private 'ospital after we leaned on 'em and they confessed they had only robbed some backstreet stores. They 'ave all been spoken to and 'ave agreed not to do any blaggins wiv out clearin' it wiv the committee first.

"Three of 'em 'ave said they will go back to their own country when they 'ave recovered. It seems that robberies ain't so regulated there as they are here."

There was a cheer from the audience. "Now, we come to the real issue here. These unregistered hoodlums, is copyin' the methods by the four greatest heist merchants we've known. The Gang of Four. Let me express my condolences that one of them died last year. Let's 'ave a minute's silence in memory of Reg Crowther, one the best sawn off-shotgun users in the business, and never 'urt anyone."

The Trio held back their tears.

After a minute, Tommy carried on. "We 'as to catch this gang that's undermining our legitimate business. We can't 'ave freelancers, who don't pay membership fees nor give us a cut of the proceeds, robbin' us of a rightful means of an income, it's a right bleedin' liberty when the fuzz keep-at us day in day out blamin' professional. We gotta do summut about it. Any ideas?"

The audience clapped and cheered.

Reggie Rudge, the leader of the South-East London Chapter, stood up and addressed his fellow blaggers. "I understand the cops haven't got a clue. I finks we've gotta help 'em bring these treacherous mob to book. I know lots of us have friendly Old Bill that we can drop info to and it'll keep us outta the frame. Wotcha say, we all becomes stoolies fer the sake of our future business. Let's 'ave a vote."

All hands were raised in agreement.

Tommy stood up and said, "Fanks all of yous, it's nice to see such solidarity. Now if yous 'as any info that help us I suggest yous lets Razor Ron here 'ave it. He'll collect all the info then we'll decide which of our cop contacts gets the dirt. Okay?"

As the Trio were returning to Bogwash by train, the colonel said he was impressed with efforts.

Lenny had been quiet for some time, then said, "Should have asked 'em to improve me pension."

The colonel responded, "Considerin' we never topped it up by givin' the Federation a cut of any of our takin's, cos we never got t'keep 'em, we're not doin' too bad."

Chapter 17

BELINDA Bennett had married her wealthy husband and retired from her job, then he'd died unexpectedly after five years of wedded bliss. She took the tenancy of the private wing at the Retreat without declaring her background. If she had, there were some occupants who would panic. It had been some weeks before any event caused problems. Matters were about to change.

Suspended Detective Inspector Bernie Bamber continued his secret investigation, he was becoming increasingly sure high-level people were protecting the Gang of Four. He was increasingly convinced that the body in the coffin weren't the remains of Reg Crowley, and someone had rigged the DNA test. His mother insisted he earned his keep by painting the outside of the windows and cut up logs for the fire.

How was he going to do his job without a warrant card? He was becoming increasingly sure top-brass were protecting the Gang of Four and were sure they knew where Reg Crowther was hiding and were part of the conspiracy to hide him. He decided he must find the evidence.

Belinda was reading a letter from a former junior colleague, now a high ranker, from her old occupation. She smiled. Good information was a godsend. She had just hit on a large vein of knowledge.

As she read the letter in her flat, colonel Guy Granger walked the footpath alongside the River Crabby recalling events in his colourful career as a bank robber, his mind wandered to thinking of who the four were masquerading as the old team.

Jock was visiting the farm to move the CD-player and loudspeakers to a new location and saw a flock of sheep were now in the field. He began playing his bagpipes resulting in the sheep running away. The farmer told him they were Dorset Horn, a rare breed. It was clear they disapproved of highland music.

After the farmer had gone, and there was no sign of the sheep, he sat on the trunk of a fallen tree and watched a large Red Deer stag walked across the field with a dozen does and offspring following. Occasionally stopping, ears twitching.

Jock's mind was miles away, he was remembering his days as an aspiring rally driver, a hotshot getaway driver for a Glasgow gang of robbers. Then being forced South by gangland bosses for 'not toeing the line and sleeping with the gangland bosses' eldest daughter. The girl's father disapproved of the liaison." The deer had disappeared when he came out of his memory trance.

He packed his bagpipes into the carry-case and headed for a dram at The *Gripe and Groan*.

In Bogwash Lenny was driving six of the Tartanettes to a rehearsal. He wasn't listening to the chatter in the back of the mini-bus. He had learned to switch off as he couldn't cope with the intellectual content.

Back at the Retreat, it was lunchtime and Henry Styles was explaining to three elderly fellow tenants how they could make an investment in a 'dead cert winner'. He waved an unlit Havana cigar around, as if to emphasise his wonderful offer. All three agreed they wanted a day or so to consider his offer.

Styles had boasted to the women that they would earn some eight percent per annum from handing over the investment to him. "I can give a binding contract with a Jersey, Channel Island, bank." He sat back, waving his large, unlit, cigar about, with his neat moustache quivering. All the women nodded as if they understood. Styles left the lounge, leaving the women chatting together. He appeared to be pleased with his sales effort.

Belinda returned to the Retreat from London at teatime and came into the lounge. One of the lady residents, who had listened to Styles, asked Belinda what she thought of the plan to invest between five and ten-thousand, 'smackers' as he called the financial amount. One of the proposed investors showed her a brochure. She read the well-prepared, full-coloured, four-page A4 literature, she frowned and handed it back, saying, "Stall him for a couple of days, tell him it takes time to arrange such a sum. I'll asked some people I know about this."

She now knew Styles' real identity. She had to embarrass him and block his activities before he did any damage.

The six o'clock TV news reported an attempted bank robbery in the Berkshire town of Bracknell, carried out by four old men, one driving the stolen getaway car. They'd fled empty handed after shooting a hole in the ceiling with a sawn-off shotgun. Security screens came down, locking them in the foyer, they escaped by smashing a window, leading to the street, it had no security screen. The colonel chuckled as he watched the broadcast, "God, they're just as bad as we were. I wonder who they are?" One of them was said to be driving the getaway car, a red Mark Two Jaguar, the TV news reported.

Joanna was having a quiet day. No language lessons going wrong and no subsequent punishment.

Martha had arrived back at Gatwick Airport and was waiting for a train to Brighton. Jock was unaware of her imminent arrival in Bogwash.

The Trio were enjoying a late afternoon drink in The *Gripe and Groan*. Returning to the Retreat, the colonel saw Minnie leap from the branch of the large oak tree onto the balcony outside his flat, then climb in through the small open window. He smiled.

The colonel entered his flat and found Minnie waiting patiently for him to empty food into a saucer. The colonel fed her then heated a ready-made meal in the microwave. As he finished the meal, a knock came at the door. Belinda was standing in the passage, she put a finger to her mouth denoting silence. She was carrying an A4 blue folder and walked past him into the flat. Minnie had done one of her vanishing acts.

He was surprised when he read the contents of the dossier. She said to him, "I want to keep all this quiet, I need your help, I'm aware of you and your two pals' background."

The colonel showed no emotion. Over a cup of tea, she outlined what she wanted him to do as discreetly as possible. She left smiling at him as she left.

He quietly closed the door and returned to the lounge to find Minnie had reappeared. He sat down on next to Minnie and said, "Well, old girl, the world is full of surprises. But I still haven't worked out her background." She flicked her tail and her lips quivered as she let out a quiet meow.

Chapter 18

NEWSPAPERS are used to getting dossiers claiming corruption. Some can be substantiated, others are often proven to be fiction. For the ***Daily Globe*** this was a dynamite of a story, just the type of scandal they enjoyed exposing. If true, it could add several thousand to the circulation figures and maybe get the top position in the Newspaper of the Year Awards. This one had a good 'smell', it contained allegations of corruption at the highest level and that a gang of bank robbers were being given protection by top judiciary. And they added to their wealth by taking a cut of the gang's haul. Bamber had decided that if his colleagues were going to ignore his 'considered allegations' he would get the press involved. This was a surprise, considering his historical hatred of the Fourth Estate who'd given him bad publicity in the past.

The paper's senior investigative journalist, Larry Garcia, was tasked with confirming or destroying the story. His preliminary chat with a senior officer of the Metropolitan Police disclosed that they believed the mystery accuser had 'flipped his lid'. The officer hinted they knew who it was because of the nature of the allegations.

In a quiet riverside hotel near Reading, Garcia met suspended Detective Bernie Bamber, he was claiming he was on sick leave. His bombastic "I am right" approach did little to endear him to the experienced journalist.

Bamber opened the chat with the statement "Now, what you've got to understand, they put me on sick leave just to keep me quiet." He went on to tell Garcia that the gang of four were still 'at it' and their story that one of them had died was a complicated plot to destroy his investigation into their activities. "They even fiddled the DNA on the body I had exhumed, and their alibis were given by those keen to support them," Bamber claimed.

"Why would this gang be supported by so many top people?" Garcia asked.

Bamber tapped the side of his nose and looked around conspiratorially and said, "This gang of four were in the pay of this group of powerful and rich people."

Garcia raised his eyebrows at this allegation and hoped his hidden tape recorder had picked up the comment. He continued to write Bamber's comments in shorthand.

The meeting lasted an hour leaving Garcia shaking his head in disbelief that a retired High Court judge, along with other top lawyers, Members of Parliament, plus a musical group dressed as gorillas and a Burlesque troupe of middle-aged women were allegedly giving false alibis for four old ex-bank robbers. It didn't make sense.

On his drive back to his Richmond, Surrey, home he pondered how he was going to explain the interview to his seniors and the newspaper's lawyers; they would, he was sure, fall about laughing at the allegations. Before he put the tale forward for publication, he would have to chat with the gorillas and the aged Burlesque troupe. This bit could be fun.

He arranged to meet the rock band and the Burlesque dancers in a Bogwash hotel. Then he would interview the lawyers and MP's supposed to be part of the conspiracy. He'd decided that he was about to expose a massive conspiracy or would see a bitter policeman sectioned under the Mental Health Act. A 'good smell of a story' had begun to turn rancid. At this early stage, he had an open mind.

He asked the newspaper's librarian to check the archives and find out as much as he could about the Gang of Four's history. Overnight, he'd worked out how much had been stolen by the earlier raids by the Four. Then, he calculated the amount nicked in the re-vamped gang of robbers that Bamber was sure was the Gang of Four 'at it again'. It seemed to him that the share out by the gang and their alleged backers would be less than £1,000 each, in total, over many years. He shook his head in disbelief and went to bed.

He had arranged to meet members of the rock band in the Sea View Hotel. He was taken aback to meet five well dressed, and well-spoken elderly men. He was further surprised to discover the men's identities and former professions.

Retired judge Sir Guy Carrington-Worth; vocalist, leader of the group and better known as the judge who had given the Trio a suspended sentence. Their last conviction.

John Watson–retired merchant, banker, drummer.

Professor Reginald Stafford–Grimes, guitarist.

Doctor Leonard Fowler–retired GP, electric keyboard. And, Sir George Carter–retired lawyer and conservative Cabinet Minister, double bass.

He was amused to discover that the five had begun their musical careers in their teens as Guy and the Gorillas and amused the audience dressed in their costumes until they were stolen, along with the instruments. After the judge confiscated the items from Lenny after the trial, the five, now in retirement, re-formed the old-style rock band and became a backing group for the Tartanettes.

After chatting to the group and confirming 'The Trio's' alibi, he drove to the Grand Hotel in Brighton. His day of surprises was far from over. He met 14 middle-aged women, one was suntanned Martha.

He managed to carefully extract information that Lenny had driven some of the troupe to rehearsals or live gigs and Jock was part of the show. It became clear to him that Jock and Lenny could not have been involved in the robberies, their alibis were solid along with those of the colonel.

He slowly introduced how Jock had become involved in the stage act. He wasn't expecting the vociferous support, particularly from Martha, who had returned from Alicante the night before. She made it clear that she believed Jock and Lenny were loyal and hardworking members of the team and had never missed an engagement.

Later, at home, he checked the dates of the raids and those gigs the Tartanettes had taken part in with Jock as part of the act and Lenny had driven part of the group to the venue. It was clear to him that the raids had taken place at locations where the two old villains were many miles away. A similar story emerged with the colonel. Why, he asked himself, would all these people lie? It didn't make sense.

He kept Bamber quiet by telling him his story was being meticulously investigated.

It was to be a week before he began looking at the allegations in a different way. He knew that the colonel, Lenny and Jock were many miles away from Staines when a post office was targeted by an elderly gang of three with a fourth at the wheel of a stolen Mark Two Jaguar. More than £30,000 was taken.

The story the Globe ran would do little to help suspended D.I. Bamber and his quest to 'nail' the gang of four.

COPYIST GANG RAIDS BANKS

A MYSTERY gang of four, dressed as old men, have baffled police by using the methods of a gang put out of business some years ago, with long jail terms.

None of the remaining three of the gang were within miles of the robbery.

Police are working on the theory that a group imitating the old gang are behind the raids.

The story went on with a statement by a senior Met officer.

Bamber read the Globe, threw the paper across the room and bellowed, "He's stitched me up. How can I expose this corruption?" He went quiet, sat down, pulled the palm of his hand down his face. "I'll get them."

On the same day, Harry Styles expressed his frustration that none of the three, elderly 'targets' had agreed to invest, Belinda Bennett was preparing to expose him. She needed the help of old friends and caught the London train.

Chapter 19

BELINDA Bennett's background was unknown to Henry Styles or anyone else in The Retreat at least for the time being, she wanted it kept that way. The colonel sat alone at the back of the lounge of The Riverside pub. A lady entered wearing a knee length raincoat, dark glasses and a scarf covering her head. All this helped disguise her.

She looked around at the near empty bar and sat down at the same table as the colonel, removing her glasses. They were sitting in a quiet part of the pub with no other customers nearby, unless they were sitting at the next table. She opened the conversation, "No one must know we are sharing information on Harold Simms, otherwise known as Henry Styles."

The colonel was slightly amused at her attempts of secrecy.

"Yes, I was able to discover his identity, thanks to underworld sources," the colonel said.

"Good, let's keep our inquiries a secret. You like being called colonel, don't you?"

"I do."

"No problems. Let's examine what we know so far before he convinces some women to invest in his scheme and disappears. We've got to expose him." She smiled at the colonel. "I understand you and your two pals have given up villainy and you earn some honest money by telling people how futile armed robbery is."

"I do that in my after-lunch speaking engagements and my proposed book. The others are involved in a show biz enterprise."

"Good," Belinda replied, then added, "I understand a wayward detective has been accusing you of being responsible for some recent robberies and he claims that some well-placed people are hiding your pal, Reg."

The colonel answered, "He won't believe he's dead, despite DNA on his exhumed body. He believed the coffin would be full of bricks and Reg is in hiding, protected by some top people. He's clearly off his trolley."

Belinda continued, "Right now, he's been suspended by the Met, pending an investigation into his activities. Let's get down to what we know about Styles, we'll deal with Bamber and his stupidity later," Belinda said.

As the two were chatting and swapping intelligence, a newly refurbished bank in Wandsworth, South London was being raided. The banking hall was empty, a silent alarm went off as steel shutters came down, locking the three inside. The three blasted a side window with their three shotguns and escaped to the street. Two squad cars had arrived outside the bank just as a dark blue Mark Two Jaguar screamed away from the scene. The robbers had fled empty handed.

None of the gang knew about the steel shutter. It was soon discovered that the car had been stolen near Oxford two days before. The car was later found abandoned near Richmond.

Chapter 20

ACTIVITIES at the Retreat ranged from the bizarre, anti-social to head shaking disbelieve. Most of these events, the Trio managed to avoid. Not all mind-boggling events occurred in the residential home. One event the colonel preferred to forget, was at a council run award ceremony for individuals becoming British citizens.

Absame Abdikarim had lived in England since the mid-1960s, arriving as a refugee from Somalia with his parents. Now, aged 58 he decided he finally wanted to be a British citizen. He had contemplated such a step soon after arriving from Somalia. He had successfully passed the criteria for being British, he wanted to do the right thing. He'd decided to change his name to an English sounding one, once he was declared a British citizen. Most who had known him for years, called him Andy and he would also change his surname to Karim.

Now, semi-retired he had befriended the Trio as customers of his shop and would occasionally join then for a drink at the *Gripe and Groan*. He would only drink one pint of Flowers Bitter.

The Trio enjoyed listening to his stories of his first days in England, setting up his first street corner store in Bogwash and how he dealt with attempts to rob his shop and dealing with youths trying to steal sweets. His eldest son now ran the twenty shops the family owned.

Andy was proud of his Somali heritage but had been trying for some years to be a citizen of the country that had given his family sanctuary decades before. Now, he had been awarded the privilege and was invited to a ceremony at Bogwash Town Hall. The invite said he could bring two members of the family or friends. Members of his family thought he was mad and refused to attend the ceremony. He asked the Trio if the two of them could give him support on his big day. On the day of the ceremony, Jock had agreed to meet his daughter in London.

Andy drove the colonel and Lenny to the ceremony. Little did they realise how many others were getting their citizen certificate and it was so 'formal'. Both had to sit at the rear of the room and weren't allowed to take pictures. Andy sat with thirty others at the front.

A large lady with an identity tag hanging around her neck told the assembled what would be happening. She then announced the officials, the Deputy Lord Lieutenant of Bogshire, Henry Purves a retired director of an animal food business who was standing in as the Queen's Representative, the Lord Lieutenant. She then introduced the mayor of Bogwash.

Percy Plumb was a diminutive man and when not dealing with council matters and mayoral duties, he drove a London-style taxicab. With a large red gown of office trailing on the floor, his chain off office came down below his stomach. Both were clearly made for a taller, bigger, person. The tricorne style black hat trimmed with large, white, Ostrich feathers virtually disguised his upper face, with a white ostrich feather incongruously attached to one side. He removed the hat and placed it on the table in front of him, exposing his baldhead and a heavy set of spectacles. Along with four others, two men and two women stood alongside them. Two on either side. The six of them sat down.

As they sat down, an attendant walked down the side of the hall and using a long pole, he opened three side windows, he told a member of the audience he'd been told to do this to lower the temperature in the room.

The large lady announced she was Gwendoline Grant, the deputy Commissioner for the district. She didn't enlarge on the deputy Commissioner of what. She introduced Henry Purves, she said was representing Her Majesty. He raised his hand and gave a slight bow. She then introduced Percy Plumb. He waved at the assembled audience, many of whom couldn't see him.

Gwendoline Grant then said the Deputy-Lieutenant would say a few words.

"Congratulations all of you, after this ceremony you will be citizens of the United Kingdom. Well done." Henry Purves sat down.

Gwendoline then announced the Mayor and stood away from the table.

Holding several A4 pages the small, rotund man, stood up. Lenny whispered to the colonel, "Is he really standing? I can hardly see him."

"Shush," the colonel responded.

Percy paused, he shuffled the pages, then slowly began. "Hello ladies and gentlemen, I'm the mayor of Bogwash." He paused and scanned his notes. "Welcome to Bogwash, the most beautiful town in England." Someone laughed.

He carried on, unfazed by the interruption. "Yes, we have a lot to offer to anyone who is a resident. You have chosen to be part of our community." He paused, looked at his notes and started again, "I have to tell you..." He paused again and studied his notes. "Bogwash welcomes you. We are a very charitable community. I do a lot of charity work."

Lenny learned over and whispered to the colonel, "He's boring."

"Shhhh," the colonel urged.

Plumb droned on. Those at the back of the hall had difficulty hearing him. After ten minutes of Plumb frequently pausing and repeating himself. Lenny's patience ran out; he couldn't understand what the Mayor was saying or hear him properly. He stood up and shouted, "Oi, pillock brain speak up, we can't hear yer."

A couple of people gave a short clap, the colonel tugged at Lenny's jacket and urged him to sit down. He responded by saying, "Well, what's the use of coming only to listen to that idiot waffling on. He doesn't make any sense, anyway."

There was a stunned silence, the mayor shuffled his papers then lay them down on the table. At this moment, a gust of wind came through the open windows. The papers were scattered across the floor. There was a scramble to recover them. The papers were pinned down and returned to the mayor, "Just a minute, I'll find were I was and continue," he declared.

He looked through the jumbled up-pages until he could find the last point he'd made. He gave up and said, "We're a caring community and look after the elderly." He stopped.

"Ah, the wrong speech. I think I'll stop." He looked at Gwendoline with an appealing look.

She announced the next part of the ceremony, each one of those who were to receive citizenship would now swear or affirm loyalty to Her Majesty Queen Elizabeth. One by one, the participants read from a card of a pre-prepared speech. The mayor could be seen trying to re-organise the pages of his speech.

Gwendoline then asked each to step forward and receive their certificate. Andy was seventh in line. Number four was a tall, elegant Brazilian girl. The mayor decided he would delay the certificate awarding ceremony. Cecil Plumb was clearly smitten with the attractive 25-year-old. His head came level with the bottom of her breast. The girl was a little taller than one and a half metres.

Lenny was irritable and in need of a pint. He shouted out, "Leave her alone yer dirty old beggar. Let's get on wiv things."

Some of the audience laughed as they turned around to see who had interrupted.

Before Lenny could say any more and any official descended on him, the colonel steered him out of the door. He said, "You're slowing things down, c'mon, we'll wait for Andy downstairs."

As they waited for the ceremony to end, they read the various activities sponsored by Bogwash council. The first to appear from the ceremony was the tall Brazilian. She spotted the colonel and Lenny and walked over to thank them, she said, "That little man in the red robe."

"The mayor, you mean?"

"Yes, him."

"My God, he is so boooring." She emphasised the 'Boring'.

"He is, how you say, a dirty old man. Thank you, for shouting out, how you say, Stopped him in his road."

"Track, you mean," the colonel corrected her.

"Yes, that. Well, thank you so much, have a nice day."

She smiled at them and walked away.

Andy arrived and gave a leap into the air and shouted, "I've done it, I've done it." He held the lower part of his back and uttered, "Oooh, I wish I hadn't done that."

Then a group of 'new' British citizens and their friends noisily walked past. They were quickly followed by Purves, Plumb, Gwendoline and the unnamed four. They studiously ignored the colonel, Lenny and Andy heading down a corridor leading to the Mayor's Parlour. The Mayor's red cloak swept the floor as he walked past, he was holding his chain of office in his hand to stop it banging against his groin as he walked.

Lenny looked at the group disappearing down the corridor, and said, "He's a short arsed, pompous pillock."

"Oh! Say what you mean Lenny, it helps," was the colonel's response.

The three then headed for the *Gripe and Groan*.

Lenny told the landlord he'd had an educational and interesting afternoon.

The landlord gave him a puzzled look and began pulling three pints of Flowers Bitter.

Jock arrived as he was pulling the second pint and said, "And mine's a large of my usual, landlord."

The landlord replied, "Don't ask, Lenny, what sort of day he's had, he's caught a dose of intelligence. I'll add your drink to this tab." Jock joined the others to find an exuberant Andy showing to, whoever was interested, his certificate.

Chapter 21

TWO days after what the colonel called the 'certificate cringe', life in the Retreat was following its usual path, the colonel had dubbed 'structured lunacy'. Both Jock and Lenny had managed to avoid the obvious demands of Prunella Pratchett. Now, aged eighty, Pru believed she was the same attractive woman she was when in her twenties.

After many lovers, she had married late in life. Her husband suddenly died on their honeymoon. Now living in the private wing of the Retreat, she decided she needed a new partner.

Anyone meeting Pru for the first time, would think this slim, demure lady appeared to be the architect of shyness and reserve. In private, she made it clear to suitable males she was interested in more than a casual chat. Jock and Lenny had managed to escape her vigorous attention.

Sitting in the lounge, reading a daily newspaper, whilst waiting for his two pals, the colonel was unconcerned about her entering the room.

Pru sat down next to the colonel and began commenting on the weather and when the cold season came, she preferred snuggling up in bed with a sturdy male. She winked at the colonel and tugged her skirt up above her knees and gave him an encouraging smile.

The colonel's face twitched, and he gave a cough. Pru carried on in her quiet voice saying, "That's been my problem in life, I've never found the right man with similar ideals. It would be nice, you know."

As he was about to reply, Lenny and Jock came into the lounge and before they could say much, he stood up and said, "C'mon we'll be late fer that meeting and steered his two pals out of the door before they could say a word to Pru.

As they walked up the road to the *Gripe and Groan* Lenny asked, "What's this important meeting?"

"Escaping from that woman," the colonel responded. He didn't enlarge why.

As Pru made her feelings known to the colonel, new tenant Cyril Carling was settling into life in the Retreat. Relying on walking aids, following a car accident, he spent his time working on his laptop computer. It was unusual to see him in the lounge.

Unperturbed by her attempts to interest the colonel, she thought Cyril could be interesting.

At the *Gripe and Groan* the colonel, Jock and Lenny pondered why an ambulance was departing the lane in which the Retreat was located.

It was the following day before they discovered that Cyril had suffered a heart attack after a conversation with Pru.

Chapter 22

HAROLD Pearson had applied for his new passport and his life with Anna was becoming lonely and frustrating. From spending most nights with her in her large bed, he had been banished to his own. "Until after the wedding," she insisted as she planned her big day and decided what the wedding feast would consist of. He had no say in the planning. His nervous facial twitch became worse. Life in the Caribbean beckoned.

He planned his best escape route, a flight to America from Gatwick, then another flight to Jamaica, or a leisurely cruise from Southampton. In Joanna's flat, she was threatening Frank Fawcett, the Merseyside-born mayor of Bogwash, with chastisement if he didn't improve his English. He had a range of words, best described as unacceptable in good society. He always read from a typewritten speech his secretary wrote for him. The little man wriggled his large posterior in anticipation, as he made every effort to get the lesson wrong. Joanna flexed her cane.

In the lounge, Henry Styles was waving a large unlit Havana cigar around as he discussed financial investments with Belinda Bennett, who nodded and made notes on a small writing pad. Henry thought this was her taking a positive interest.

Their chat was interrupted with a large howl from what was clearly a male voice. Both headed for the door leading to the corridor. They were confronted by the warden, Stella Stern, sitting in an armchair with her head in her hands and crying out "Oh my God, oh, my God" over and over. It was her first day back at the Retreat after receiving counselling from a psychologist.

Lying on the floor, clutching his genitals, was Paul Planter the newly released psychiatric patient, he was stark naked, and was uttering between clenched teeth, "God, it stings, it stings."

Standing alongside was Brenda Bates, clutching an empty glass tumbler, she was swaying unsteadily and laughing out loud, finally saying in a slurred manner, "That deflated him, that did. I took the rise out of him." She slumped into an armchair and appeared to be asleep, still clutching the glass tumbler.

It transpired that Ernest had tried to tell Stella he knew he was a ghost and no one could see him. Stella had collapsed in the armchair at the sight of him just as Brenda staggered into view with a nearly full tumbler of whisky. She promptly tossed it over Paul's 'ready for action' nether region and kicked him where it hurt most.

As the scene began, Jock entered the building holding his bagpipes. He looked down at Paul and smelt whisky and commented, "Aye, he's a man, a man fer all that, what a waste of guid whisky," then wandered away. Henry and Belinda tried to calm Stella down and persuade Paul to make himself respectable and stop holding his privates. Brenda was enjoying her alcohol induced slumber.

An ambulance took Paul away and paramedics tended to Stella who was then admitted to the lady's section of the same psychiatric establishment as Paul.

As they watched her being helped into the ambulance a large, bald headed, man with a smile on his face was leaving the building. He was rubbing his posterior as he walked up the road to the car park. He was seen wincing as he sat in the driver's seat.

Henry Styles didn't finish his sales spiel with Belinda.

Unusually, the Trio knew nothing of this incident until told hours later.

Chapter 23

THE TRIO were spending less time together with Jock rehearsing his highlander display with the Tartanettes, Lenny was remaining secretive about his activities when not driving the dancers. The colonel worked on his memoires and giving talks on his time as a top planner and active bank robber.

He was enjoying telling of his life as a failed robber and how his 'well thought out' plans invariably led to the Gang of Four's arrest. He discovered his audiences of the legal profession and police, appreciated his tales of failure and the usual trials and prison sentences. He was now earning more than any bank or post office heist he'd ever been involved in.

Jock was taking to being something in show biz and would return from his latest gig and give any residents in the lounge a display of his talents. This was usually fuelled with his flask of whisky he carried in his sporran.

The colonel and Lenny were not always nearby to rescue him in his tipsy state and deny residents of a rendition of his latest jokes and Scottish music. On this day, he arrived back from rehearsals carrying his bagpipes and his language delivery affected by his intake of whisky. The colonel and Lenny were nowhere to be seen.

There were more residents in the lounge than usual following a local charity holding a sales bazaar. In full highland regalia, his usual stage costume, he swept into the room. In a slurred tone, he gave his version of the Skye boat song.

I've just got doon from the Isle of Skye
I'm nae very big and I'm awfuy shy
The ladies shout as I go by
Donald where's your troosers.

Let the winds blow high,
Let the winds blow low,
Doon the street in my kilt I go
And all the ladies say hello
Donald where's your troosers.

A lady took me to a ball
And it was slippery in the hall
I was afraid that I would fall
'Cause I didnae have on my troosers.

They'd like to wed me everyone
Just let them catch me if they can
You canna put the brakes on a highland man
Who doesn't like wearing troosers.

To wear the kilt is my delight,
It isn't wrong, I know it's right.
The highlanders would get a fright
If they saw me in troosers.

Well, I caught a cold and m'nose was raw
I had no hankie at all
So I hiked up my kilt and I gave it a blow,
Now you cannae d'that with troosers.

Some of his audience managed to sneak out, a couple of other fell asleep. After a few verses, he ended his rendition and begun the first line of a ditty…

A well-endowed barmaid from Leuchers…

He hadn't begun the second line when the colonel and Lenny walked in and tried to steer him out of the door. One old man, pushing a four-wheeled walking aid, blocked the exit. Jock didn't finish his original verse and began to deliver a rendition of another ditty.

There was a young lady of Dunblane
Who fancied it now and again
And again and again
Again and again
Again and again and again.

His voice went up and down in a theatrical manner. The colonel and Lenny waited until he'd finished and steered him from the room. Lenny picked up the bagpipes before anyone could complain about their action.

Jock could still be heard shouting out a ditty as they persuaded him to enter lift.

They managed to propel him into his room. He promptly collapsed on the bed and fell asleep, still dressed in full highland regalia, holding his pipes across his stomach.

As the two were preparing to leave Jock's room, the colonel looked out of the window and muttered, "Oh God, the ghost's back."

An ambulance crew was wheeling Paul Planter into the building, he was waving amiably at passers and saying, "I'm a recovered ghost." Those who didn't know him, looked on bewildered. The colonel slowly added, "The apparition returns."

Lenny had joined him at the window and added, "Until next 'auntin."

The colonel smiled as they let themselves out of the flat, leaving Jock snoring loudly.

The two returned to the lounge to find many had left, Henry Styles was in deep conversation with Belinda Bennet. Lenny looked at Styles and said, "Roger Moore, that's who that is, y'know the James Bond actor. That's who that is. Why would he slum it here with his wealth?"

As the two made their way back to their respective rooms, the colonel quietly said to Lenny, "Can't be Roger Moore, he died some time ago."

"Dead?" Lenny said with some puzzlement. "Nobody told me, it could be his ghost, y'know."

"Go to bed Lenny, I've enough of ghosts for one day. Mister Moore is no more and that fella ain't his apparition."

Lenny went into his room pondering on what an apparition was. Better speech pattern. Maybe! Intellectual improvement. Doubtful.

Elsewhere in the Retreat, the solicitor James Johnson, was biting into his handkerchief to supress his groans as the sting of the cane caused him to wriggle as Joanna vent her annoyance on his bare backside.

He left the building with a smile on his face. It was the best spanking he'd ever had.

Back at the Retreat, Joanna was beginning to think that her clients would never learn good English and just came to her to be chastised. What should she do? She poured herself a large sherry to help her decide.

In the *Gripe and Groan,* Lenny was telling the colonel and Jock that Belinda was really retired actress, Joan Lumsden. The colonel smiled and wondered who Lenny was confusing her with. Jock shrugged his shoulders as the colonel shook his head as Lenny went to the bar to refill their glasses.

Lenny became annoyed when the colonel suggested he was wrong and Belinda Bennett was her real name and she wasn't an actress.

"Don't talk nonsense, she just wants to hide, yer know, in coggy."

"Yer mean incognito, in disguise," the colonel suggested.

"Yeah, that's right' Lenny replied. They finished their drinks in peace. Lenny believed Belinda was in disguise. Jock simply ignored Lenny's, 'I know fer sure' approach and sipped his whisky. The colonel remained quiet.

Chapter 24

SOON after launching, Celia Worthy's courses at the University of Bogwash were attracting record numbers of young women and those long married.

Demos against these courses by boyfriends, newlywed husbands and those with a 'few years under their belt' had dwindled to the occasional frustrated spouse, who was inevitably carried away, by paramedics, from the University entrance in a state of shock.

Bogwash Hospital's reported there had been a fall in cases involving injuries to men and the police were frustrated that none of the complainants could be persuaded to press charges.

The professor sat in the *Gripe and Groan* and showed the Trio his draft of a counter curriculum entitled: ***Teaching the wife the right way.***

The colonel glanced over the A4 sheet and said, "Believe in living dangerously, don't you?"

Jock snatched the paper from him. The first section was headed, '**Men, stand firm. Know your rights.**'

He was aware the professor had never been married or in a 'domestic' arrangement with a woman.

Jock scanned the 'rules' quickly before handing the sheets back to the professor and telling Lenny he'd explain later. He knew Lenny would be confused if he read it.

The 'rules' read:

1. Ensure the new wife knows who is boss. The man is the final arbiter in all matters.
2. If she argues, threaten to reduce her personal allowance.
3. Monday is washing and ironing day (if she works, this can be re-assigned for Saturday or Sunday). Ensure she doesn't hang her smalls out at the same time as yours. Embarrassing for you.
4. From the beginning, train her to have your breakfast cooked before she leaves for work.
5. Ensure she clearly understands the meaning of conjugal rights. Complaints of headaches are not acceptable.
6. The rule is that she is home by six o'clock to cook dinner. This rule must be followed.
7. She MUST NOT show displeasure when he chooses to have an early evening 'snifter' with his pals and arrives home to a ruined dinner after closing time. She must understand this is a man's behavioural right.
8. It is his absolute right to spend the weekend watching (or playing) rugby, football, cricket or any other spectator sport, including darts and snooker.
9. She does not challenge the length of time he spends at the golf club.
10. She MUST be available to deal with rising frustration on demand.

Jock's only remark to the professor was, "Suicidal, are you?"

"What do you mean, suicidal?" he asked as he tugged at his wispy white beard and dragged his hand through his shoulder lengthy mass of untidy grey hair. He looked crestfallen as he pushed his rimless glasses to the base of his nose.

Lenny looked to the colonel for an explanation. He got no response and sat with a puzzled expression on his face.

The colonel responded by saying slowly, "This is not sensible, as Jock suggested, it's suicidal."

The professor admitted he'd assembled the suggestions following discussions with men, who had recently been married, and one who was already living back with his mother. The ideas were just an outline.

He declared his plan was to counter the success of Celia Worthy.

The Trio left the professor scanning his paper to see how he could improve the course content.

A week later, the Trio were walking past the University from a shopping expedition on the way to the *Gripe and Groan* when they confronted a large crowd of woman carrying placards.

Lynch the
Sexist Professor

Sexism
Out

Ban
Men
From
Your
Bed

Two dozen policemen surrounded the professor as they led him to a car. Many eggs were thrown and women were shouting anti-men slogans, many shouted suggestions what should be done with their manhood. Jock commented that there were no police woman to be seen.

The three, sought refuge in a shop doorway until the professor had been driven away and the crowd of women dispersed.

Soon after arriving in the *Gripe and Groan,* they were joined by their police chum, Sergeant Wallace in plain clothes. He begun bemoaning the role of women police. "Get a demo and they go into hiding."

It transpired that the contingent of female offices at Bogwash nick had refused to turn out to help control the demo. "Rebellion, that's what it is. Rebellion." He took a deep gulp of his pint of bitter. "As for that professor bloke, he needs locking up for his own protection. Gotta be of his trolley for suggesting married women should obey a quirky set of rules. Got eggs stains over me tunic for the second time this week. He's gotta be stopped. Me missus was one of those carrying a placard. Embarrassin' it was."

He took another gulp of beer and smiled, "At least the Chief Inspector's new wife was part of the demo. Funny it was when two, out of area, constables dragged her away screamin. Don't fancy his chances at home tonight. I'm stayin' with a pal for safety reasons. Now, how are you lot?"

Lenny was the first to comment, "Can't have woman tellin' me what to do."

Jock responded in rare understandable English, "You've never managed to keep one long enough to cope with the female mind."

The colonel stroked his moustache and rubbed the side of his broken nose saying, "Damned dangerous, arguin' with wimmin. Damned dangerous."

On the way back to the Retreat, Lenny pursed his lips and gave a quizzical look as he commented, "Don't unnerstand what all the fuss is about, just ignore 'em, I say, and they fall into line."

Jock slowly replied, "Yes, Lenny, if y'say so."

The colonel shook his head as they entered the building. Minnie jumped from the tree onto the balcony and through the open window into his flat.

Chapter 25

MANY of the residence had lived in the Retreat for years and enjoyed the peace, tranquillity and rays of the early morning sunshine. This idyll, of the street, was in their view, about to be destroyed.

On the opposite side of Trinity Road, a large two-floor office block had been built in the 1950s. The area had been sold by the Church after complaints of their plans to extend the graveyard. Peace had prevailed for years between the residents and the owners, a wholesale car parts enterprise. The business went bankrupt and the new owners wanted to add two more floors to the building and create a small office complex with a convenience store and a book-maker's shop at floor level. They also planned to move and extend the car park with a new entrance opposite the front door of the Retreat.

Members of the planning committee liked the idea. This could have been influenced by the meetings held in an expensive Bogwash restaurant, all paid for by the developers.

With an effort to win over the residents of the Retreat, a public relation exercise was organised jointly by the owners, architects and developers. They would explain the concept and provide a free fish and chips luncheon.

What was thought of as a well-planned PR effort, was about to become a fiasco.

Twenty-six tenants turned up to hear what the plans were. Ten members representing the owner's proposal laid out a table with a large board showing carefully cut out polystyrene representatives of each building in the street and the shape of the new look spare parts building. A pretty girl smiled at each tenant of the Retreat as she handed out a glossy brochure showing elegantly drawn colour montages of the building.

All was quiet until the colonel asked, "Tell me, have you applied and been granted planning permission?"

One of the developer's team stepped forward and in his class-ridden accent, said very slowly, as he spoke to the colonel, "You must understand, we are looking for your support in this concept, then you can be proud that you helped create the idea." He smiled as if he had said something very important and sat down.

One of the other tenants raised his arm. "Do tell, who are you, and what position do you hold?"

The tall, well-dressed man stood up and gently smiled, saying, "Sir George Lucas, I'm chairman of Con Construction."

Someone in the background was heard to loudly comment, "Sounds right t'me, con b'name, con b'nature."

Sir George ignored the comment and sat down.

A younger man sitting next to Sir George stood up holding what appeared to be a snooker cue and pointed at the board with the cut out stuck-on polystyrene representatives of the old and new buildings in the street. Telling the assembled tenants, "You will see how carefully we have blended the new building into the elegance of the older one." There came a ripple of laughter from the audience.

The young man looked around nervously. Other members of the team looked at each other nervously.

Sir George stood up and without effort smiled at the group of elderly tenants and said, "At Con Construction, we aim to provide elegant solutions to solve local problems, we feel this design fits the bill…"

His voice faded away as a loud ripple of laughter rent the air and another member of the audience shouted out, "Yeah yer name suits, Con Construction. Yer con yer clients, con the council, con the public."

The smile faded from Sir George's face as he pushed paperwork into a brief case and without saying a word strode out of the room. As he did so, one of the audience stood up, walked towards the table, raised his heavy walking stick and brought it crashing down of the model of the scheme. The board split in two and polystyrene bits flew across the room. Thus, ended the first lesson, as the audience quietly filed out of the room, leaving young lady members of the presentation team to rescue the bits of the mock buildings and the broken board and leave.

The colonel chuckled, turned to Lenny and Jock and said, "I'm sure he is a bigger crook than we ever were."

Lenny and Jock laughed with Jock adding, "Legal robbery."

Belinda Bennett pursed her lips and made copious notes in her notebook.

Chapter 26

THE Retreat was unusual in the residential home business. It was, effectively, two types of self-help homes for the retired. One part of the large building was for those residents that could afford to pay the rent. The other part was for social help residents, the rent paid for by the council. The gardens and lounge were used by both.

One part of the lounge was used by the private tenants these were mainly elderly ladies, living of the monies their late husbands had left them. The other part was occupied by those on benefits and a small number fresh out of serving time in prison for a variety of crimes. Rarely did they mix. The same applied to the garden.

The only time the social divide was ignored was the weekly bingo session or when a second-rate comedian, a ventriloquist with a speech impediment, or the best part, an intoxicate singer, male or female, were brought in to entertain. By the end of the evening, it was not unusual for the audience to have fallen asleep. This one night was a rare occasion when the tenants cheered and clapped the singer at the end of his act. His comical efforts were ignored by tenants.

Liam O'Leary specialised in presenting an act emulating his favourite American rock and roll star, Elvis Presley. The

Irishman appeared on the small stage copying the singer's dress code and large quiff. As he walked onto stage, he placed a large glass of amber liquid on a small table. He twanged his guitar and broke into a rendition of *Hound Dog.*

By the time he was half-way through his interpretation of *Blue Suede Shoes,* the mixed audience had dozed off. At the end of each song, a youth ran onto stage carrying a bottle of teacher's whisky and topped up the singer's glass. He broke into his version of *Jailhouse Rock* after taking a gulp of the amber liquid. His singing delivery was now becoming unintelligible and his guitar playing out of tune, he swayed. He never finished the song. There was a pause. He took another gulp from the glass. Swayed again, then in slow motion he fell over, still clutching his guitar and the half-empty glass. Not a drop of whisky was spilled as the youth ran on stage and rescued the drink, leaving a comatose Liam O'Leary lying where he'd fallen.

There was a pause and the audience woke-up, cheered and clapped. Liam slept on.

It was a rare event when both social classes enjoyed the same stage act.

Jock commented later. "The man himself was bad enough, wanting to copy The King, that Liam fella must be off his trolley."

"So, you're not an Elvis fan, then?" the colonel asked.

Chapter 27

A COUPLE of days later, the Tartanettes were practicing their burlesque routine in the church hall at St Jaspers. There was no sign of the skimpy tartan costumes they wore for their live acts all the middle-aged ladies were dressed in leotards. Jock was missing, he'd gone to practice in the wood alongside the farm where he'd wooed the herd of Ayrshires. The herd had been moved to another field. Jock began to give a go at playing 'Scotland the Brave' on his bagpipes. He'd just begun his second attempt to get it right when he looked up. Standing at the fence, separating the field from the wood were ten shaggy-haired cattle with long horns, they were stamping their feet in keeping with the tune and swaying from side-to-side. There were no signs of any sheep.

Jock switched to a non-descript highland melody and the cattle swayed their head from side to side. It seemed as if they were enjoying his efforts.

As he walked back to the Retreat, he met the farmer. After a chat, he discovered his new bovine audience were young Highland beef cattle. He continued his walk and chuckled and muttered, "Aye, good Scots coos, respect fer fine music."

Back at the church hall, the troupe admitted they were missing one of their star members. Walking along the bank of the River Boggy, the colonel wondered if he would ever see the blonde bombshell again. He realised he'd developed a soft spot for Harriet St Claire, who'd gone to Canada to help her sick sister and said she may not return.

He wrote a note in his pocketbook about one of his failed robberies. He would expand on the story when he got home. He was beginning to enjoy reminiscing about his failures as, in his mind, a big shot armed robber. He was also thinking how he could undermine Con Construction's plans.

The same morning, Joanna Creswell placed an advert in the *Bogwash Bugle* saying she was suspending English lessons until further notice. Following its publication, she departed on a holiday, telling no one her destination.

At lunchtime, the colonel, Lenny and Jock strode up the road to The *Gripe and Groan* pub, they met another elderly man outside and went in. In the distance, Bernie Bamber sat in his car and peered through binoculars. He was convinced they had met up with the elusive Reg. He sat in the car for over an hour until he saw the four leave the pub. They stood chatting for a couple of minutes, he took a long-lens photograph of the group, one of whom he believed was Reg, turn towards town. The other three walked away in the opposite direction. He didn't question why the man he believed was Reg strode away without the use of a walking aid.

He followed the man to the railway station and saw him board a Southampton bound train. In the Railway Tavern, Bamber sent a text message to the ever-suffering police sergeant, who was still willing to help him, that he needed to see the last known pictures of the gang of four.

At the *Gripe and Groan,* the colonel announce that when he'd finished his book, *Confession of a Bank Robber,* he was going to work on another telling of other heist merchants in the industry. "Some were as hopeless as we were. I think I'll call it *Failed heister's.*"

No one made any comment and Lenny headed for the bar and a refill.

Chapter 28

JOCK'S language usually became understandable after a few 'we drams'. His consumption of whisky hadn't dropped after Reg's death and his use of words, he claimed to be Gaelic, continued to confuse. Even those who could speak the ancient Scots' language, were baffled by his delivery. With a quantity of whisky consumed, he enjoyed entertaining other residents with a range of what he thought were amusing five-line ditties, all delivered in understandable English with a Scots dialect. After many months, the tenants knew the collection. He would also deliver a range of Scottish songs in his fine tenor voice, departing the lounge playing his bagpipes.

Long-time tenants acknowledged his attempts at entertaining them and usually slept through his efforts. Newcomers were becoming used to his singing, bagpipe playing and rendition of silly ditties. All the tenants, who witnessed his efforts, wished he would give them some fresh content. The reality was that these were the only ditties, songs and bagpipe tunes he knew.

None of the audience were aware that he'd borrowed the ditties from the book, Cannae Sutra by Rupert Besley. He'd discovered the book in the prison library at the beginning of his last jail sentence; he smuggled the book out when he was released.

Jock had been at a full-dress rehearsal with the Tartanettes and the rock band Guy and Gorillas. The whole cast had enjoyed drinks at a Bogwash pub after their session. He was still dressed in full highland dress when he strode in the resident's lounge at the Retreat. "Well 'ello kiddies, yer doin' alright?" No one answered, they knew what was coming.

"Bored, are ye? Then I'll cheer thee up." Without pausing, he began, "I should warn ye all, yer should never ask a Scotsman about his underwear when he's wearin' a kilt. There's a risk he may just show ye." He chuckled at his own humour and broke into a ditty, some older tenants joined in.

The good folk of Grantown-on-Spey
Make love in the time-honoured way
In bed before sleep
With a favourite sheep
Or a ram in the case of a gay.

A couple of men laughed, Belinda Bennett and the other women sat in stony silence.

Jock then began on another batch of ditties. Everyone had been aired previously.

A well-endowed barmaid from Leuchers
Had breast sticking out like bazookas
To admirers–and knockers
She explained that her knockers
Owed all to her fondness of Deuchars

Beer drinking purist will know Deuchers is a Highland brewed beverage. Without hesitation, Jock started another ditty, the audience had heard it before.

There was a young lady of Dunblane
Who fancied it now and again
And again and again
Again and again
Again and again and again.

Jock was about to begin a third ditty, he took a swig of whisky from the half-bottle he kept in his sporran then picked up his bagpipes; the colonel and Lenny arrived. They didn't give him time to begin another ditty, play his bagpipes or sing to the others. He was hustled out of the lounge and pushed into the lift, complaining loudly.

One of the male residents quietly asked, "I wonder what the third nonsense would have been?"

"At least we didn't have to hear that noise from that bag thing," another added.

The colonel and Lenny left Jock lying on his bed cuddling his bagpipes. He fell asleep as they left. The two stood outside the colonel's room, Lenny was the first to say anything, "Pity, we can't persuade him to cut out the whisky."

The colonel commented, "Oh, yeah then we won't understand a word he says."

Lenny opened the door to his flat, turned to look at the colonel and said, "That lingo of 'is caused some problems. D'yer remember that time we were nicked by a Scots cop working in the Met. Lenny broke into that mickey mouse talkin." The cop asked him what the language was, and he said it was Gaelic. The cop laughed and said it wuz more like applied gibberish. It turned out the cop could speak proper Gaelic.

The colonel laughed as he made his way to his own room and the attention of Minnie.

Chapter 29

SOME days later, the colonel was walking slowly along the Boggy riverbank on his way to the police station to meet up with Sergeant Wallace. He'd reached a narrow part of the footpath, on his right side a tall brick wall, on his left, a narrow grass bank, then the river.

His thoughts were interrupted when behind him, a female voice called, "Excuse me." He turned and saw a teenager walking along leading a large dapple-grey horse. He stepped to one side, with the river only a few feet away. Attached to the wall were three signs each, with a red circle and line. They depicted a cyclist, a scooter and a horse and rider. Under each, in black, were the warnings. **Do not ride**.

As the horse passed him and the girl said, "Thank you," he turned and continued his walk. The girl and the horse were only a few feet away when a loud voice shouted, "Get outa the way." He turned in time to see a cyclist, riding at speed, approaching. His gammy leg prevented him moving quickly. The cyclist mounted the grass verge between the tarmac covered footpath and the narrow grassy slope leading to the river. The girl and the horse had stopped. There was an anguished cry and a loud splash. It appeared the cyclist had skidded on the grass.

He looked down to see a policeman, with his helmet still in place, sitting in the shallow waters of the river, his cycle lay in the water beside him.

He struggled out of the river without help, dragging his bike onto the grassy bank. The girl was giggling. The horse let out a loud neigh as if it, too, was amused.

The constable dug into his tunic and pulled out a struggling fish and threw it into the river. Pulling himself up to his full five-foot-eleven, still dripping with water, he bellowed, "You got in my way, you impeded me in my duty."

The girl stood with her horse, still laughing. The horse shook its head and snorted. The colonel pointed to the three signs, to which the constable replied angrily and said, "That doesn't apply to the police. You're nicked." He then handcuffed the colonel, telling the girl she was a witness. He didn't ask for her name or address. The colonel protested it wasn't an offence that he could be arrested for. The constable ignored him and pushed his police issued bike to the nick, still dripping water.

At the custody desk, he told the PC on duty that he wanted the colonel charged with impeding the police and assault. Water dripped on the floor leaving a pool at his feet. Before he could continue the check in procedure or the colonel could say his piece, a loud female voice bellowed, "I've just washed that, look at the mess you've made, you damned idiot. Now, you can clear up the mess." She thrust a mop and bucket in the hapless young constable's hand.

The colonel, still in handcuffs, was leaning on the counter as Sergeant Wallace emerged from a rear office wondering what the noise was, particularly from the cleaning lady. The colonel was quick to say to the sergeant, "Nicked me fer riding his bike into the river from the footpath," and smiled at Wallace, holding up handcuffed wrists, who then ordered them to be removed.

An angry Doreen Dabble stood and watched the dripping constable and the pool of water at his feet. She had just cleaned the floor. She thrust a mop and bucket into his hands and told him to clear the mess.

Police constable Stanley Simkins stood with bucket and mop in his hand still dripping water. He wriggled and put the cleaning items down, or rather dropped them. Sergeant Wallace had carried a glass of water in with him when he heard the commotion. He put it down on the counter. Simkins dug into the front of his tunic and pulled out a small crab. Wallace, without saying a word, held his hand out. Simkins deposited the wriggling creature in his open palm. Wallace, without saying a word, dropped it into the glass of water.

Simkins continued telling the sergeant, "This man and a girl leading a white horse."

"Dapple grey," the colonel quickly corrected him. "It was dapple grey."

A large pool of water had gathered around Simkins' feet. The sergeant leaned on the counter, holding his hands together. "There was no reason for you to be riding on the footpath, despite you being a constable. There are signs clearly stating no riding, cycles, scooters or horses; that is why the girl was walking the horse. It seems to me that you ended up in the water, was a touch of rough justice. Now, where's the colonel's walking stick?"

Simkins stepped back and picked up a walking stick he'd place on chairs at the rear of the room.

The sergeant straightened up, "Well, colonel, we planned a chat. Let me get my sports jacket and we'll have that pint."

Simkins was about to leave to change out of his wet uniform when Chief Inspector Solly Salmon walked into the room. "Who's the constable who arrested an elderly man walking along a path and nearly ran into my daughter and her horse?"

The constable manning the reception desk quietly pointed to Simkins.

"My office, NOW!" he bellowed at the still dripping rooky constable carrying the mop and bucket.

Later in the pub, Wallace wanted to know whether he'd heard anymore from Bamber.

"So far, all is quiet," the colonel replied.

Chapter 30

A FEW days after this episode, the colonel and Jock sat in the *Gripe and Groan* waiting for Lenny to join them. The colonel had been for a riverside walk thinking about his memoirs, Lenny had been with the Tartanettes preparing for a major show in Birmingham.

Lenny arrived in an exuberant mood telling his two pals he was looking forward to seeing a new series about the police where the inspector was a real buffoon, never listening to what his staff were saying.

"I've just been watching some of the publicity. I'd been watching that Midsomer Murder programme. Great series that. Plenty of murders, that fella Barnaby always sorts it out." He enthused before ordering a pint.

"So, what's this new series that's coming up?" The colonel asked.

"It's seems it's all about savin' the Special cops."

"They're not called that now, they're Community Police," Jock commented.

Lenny tapped the side of his nose and continued, "I fink it's about how fings wuz. Yer know, before they changed."

"Sounds interesting," the colonel added. Not a big TV watching fan, he had little interest. Jock sipped his whisky and asked, "What's this new series called, Lenny? Just in case I wanna watch it."

"There runnin' adverts for it," Lenny expanded.

"Don't yer mean trailers?" Jock commented.

"It's got nuffink t'do wiv lorries and fings. It's just tellin' folks whats comin'.""

"That's a trailer," the colonel added. Lenny looked puzzled.

"Anyways, they show this stuff about an Inspector who gets fings wrong and his sarge had t'keep puttin' him right. Or if the sarge says summit the inspector gets it wrong. Sound a good series to 'me.

"What's this great series called?

"Forgot, anyway its abart savin' the old-style copper on the beat, at least I think so."

"When yer remember what it's called, let us know. Now, get us a re-fill, it's your round, punishment fer bein' late'

As Lenny was at the bar Jock commented to the colonel, "I've got a funny feelin' this new series ain't what he thinks it is."

"You're probably, right. He usually muddles things up." Lenny arrived back with a round of drinks still enthused about the new crime series.

The colonel looked at Jock and gently shook his head.

Chapter 31

THERE are many different personalities in any residential home, most want a quiet life, others make their presence known, the third group are the secret rebels. One such lady that fitted the category of ignoring the usual social norms, was Cynthia Fuller aged 82. Those who had known her for some years described her as, 'Beyond belief'. By the time she was 55, she had divorced two husbands, the third had died in bed on their honeymoon.

From that time, until she was in her late seventies, she had a string of short-time boyfriends. She then moved into the private wing of the Retreat. Within weeks, she had made a play for retired accountant Roy Grimes. Using one of her well-worn phrases, "Come up and see me sometime and I'll make you a cuppa," accompanied with a knowing wink.

No one knows for sure what happened when he took up her cheeky offer. He told the ambulance crew treating him for a heart attack before taking him to hospital about what had happened. He went to her flat and she went into the bedroom and came out soon after without clothing, "Absolute starkers, she was." According to him she invited him to her bed for a 'good time'. His heart gave out before he got there.

Three weeks later, retired postman Jim Jolley took on the tenancy of a flat in the social wing. Aged 69, he'd just lost his beloved wife of 35 years. Cynthia met him in the lounge and liked what she saw. Jim was still fit and handsome. She was a little more direct with her desires. The next day, the temporary warden noticed Jim wasn't in his flat. He wasn't answering the intercom to check his well-being. She then began opening the mail before checking if he was alright. She found one letter from Jim saying he was staying with his daughter and would send for his belongings. It later transpired, Cynthia had made an offer, she said, no normal man would normally refuse. She thought he'd 'lost his marbles'.

The colonel had managed to avoid any contact with Cynthia, until one day, both Lenny and Jock were late meeting him in the lounge. Cynthia walked into the lounge dressed in a low-cut blouse, which exposed her ample cleavage and a tight skirt with the hem just above her knees. She had lost the ability to put her bright red lipstick on without smudging.
She was quick to introduce herself to the colonel. "Well, hello, I'm Cynthia. You live here?" she asked.

"Maybe," he replied.
She tugged at the bottom of her blouse, the effect was to show even more of her cleavage and the top of a pink lacy bra. She crossed her legs exposing her upper right thigh and the bottom of lacy pink panties. She made little effort to be coy.

As she was about to continue, the door to the outside passage opened and Larry and Jock walked in. She remained quiet as the colonel stood up and the three left the room.

"Cor, she's a bit tarty, ain't she?" Lenny said as they walked to The *Gripe and Groan*.

"Yeah," the colonel replied. "It's that Fuller woman from number twelve."

Jock commented, "Still wants it, best on her own her, less dangerous."

No one replied.

Many of the elderly men at the Retreat and a nearby social club, managed to avoid her predatory approach. She continued her quest with amusing results.

Chapter 32

A FEW day later in the *Gripe and Groan,* the colonel penned a few notes. As he remembered his past, he was thinking of his time running his training company. Jock and Lenny were at rehearsals with the Tartanettes. Sergeant Craig Wallace arrived in the bar and joined him. "Just finished m'shift. On the way home. Thought I'd have a pint." He said as he settled in a chair opposite the colonel.

"Still working on your book?" The sergeant questioned.

"Getting on with it. Quiet enjoying the memories. I'm working on the part where we trained blaggers. I've already given a brief talk about that period when I owned the training company which got me and the boys banged up for the last time, I'm just expanding it for the book. It was the longest period we'd spent on the outside. We made a lot of money from the enterprise, more than we ever did from blaggin' banks and suchlike.

"We only got caught because of an undercover operation by the Met. I've never discovered who their man, or woman, was that infiltrated our courses.

"One thing I'm proud of, is that none of our pupils ever did a heist and hurt anyone.

The sergeant stood up and pointed to the colonel's empty glass, "Refill?"

"Sure, a pint of Flowers, please."

Wallace returned and asked, "Is there any truth that you banned that north London mob, the Grimbles?"

"Oh, that lot, they were a bad lot. They tried to infiltrate our courses. Thankfully, they were spotted. They wanted to steal our ideas and control villainy in the capital. I wasn't going to have that." He smiled.

"I seem to remember they were caught in a very strange way. Delivered to us, according to Dad, who was stationed at Hounslow at the time," Wallace commented.

The colonel smiled, "That mob can't do us any harm now. They're all dead. They feature as one of the stories in my book," he leaned towards Wallace and said, "I can tell how we did it. Delivered to Old Bill in style, they were."

"Go on," Wallace urged him.

The colonel laughed, "Grimble and his mob were greedy, they wanted everything. I made him an offer he couldn't refuse and described the venue as secret and highly secure. I had hired a large shipping container and had it parked in a lay-by near Heathrow. In the back we organised a table and piled up some items, like gold bars, then suggested them as a bribe to keep him off our backs. True to form he and his mob wanted to see what we were offering.

"We'd discovered where he'd hidden the spoils of a raid of a London security vault. We acquired them, well nicked 'en, before they discovered their loss. Greedy as they were, they piled-up at the container to see what we were offering. In they went, we banged the doors shut and locked the six of 'em in. The gold they'd nicked was elegantly displayed on a table.

"The next bit was straight out of a comedy. We knew your lot were looking for the robbers of the gold and other heists. We had the container lifted onto a wagon, drove it to a pub car park, some renovation work was under way and was still open for business and just a few yards from the nick. We then drove the truck away.

"We stuck a note on the door, warning the cops there were armed men inside. Along with the proceeds of armed bullion robberies and we sat in the pub and watched events. We'd sent in a motor cyclist to hand over a letter at the front desk of the nick telling about the container.

"Their banging on the inside of the steel container could be heard in the pub. The cops kept inquisitive onlookers away and surrounded the container with armed police.

"Yer should have seen them six's face when the container wuz opened and they were facin' all those police guns." The colonel laughed at the memory.

Wallace commented, "I remember Dad telling about the incident, he was based at Hounslow nick at the time. Grimble and his mob believed they had been set-up by up by the cops and they knew nothing about the gold bars. At their trial, it was disclosed that their fingerprints were found all over those gold bars and other items found in the container. They claimed they didn't know how the items got into the container."

The colonel went on, "Now, I can say what 'appened 'cos the whole of the gang are now dead. As I've said before, the dead can't sue or seek revenge."

"There are those who think otherwise, like a spirit, would you?" Wallace asked with a smile on his face and headed for the bar.

Lenny spotted someone he recognised and wandered off to have a chat. The colonel turned to Wallace and said, "He's got a right bee in his bonnet about some trailers they're showing for a new crime series in which the inspector muddles up what people say to him. According to Lenny, this inspector tells his sergeant that he's got a prisoner to sing a lullaby. When he wuz checkin' his alibi. Then another one where he was sitting in the car and had just taken a bite out of a burger when the sergeant says the crime must be a cat burglar. The inspector promptly throws his burger out of the window thinking he was eatin' a cat burger."

Sergeant Craig Wallace burst out laughing. "The idiot. It sounds like a series of adverts for hearing aids run by those people who do the eye checks, Specsavers."

"Gawd, he finks it's summut to do wiv savin' the police specials."

"Don't say anything, you could keep this goin's for some time. You know what he's like with mixing up people with film and television stars."

"We've got one of them right now, finks that new tenant Belinda Bennett, is someone called Josie Lumsden, a retired television star in disguise."

"Anyway, all that aside, what are you saying about your last heist, the Bogwash post office?" Wallace asked.

"Nuthin, never 'appened, Just doin' summit to write about. No intention of blaggin' the place," the colonel replied.

"If you say so, just a heist denied," Wallace added.

Chapter 33

THE TRIO managed to steer clear of Cynthia Fuller, as it had been suggested she was on the hunt for a new husband or live-in boyfriend, preferably younger than her and athletic in bed. She tried to behave as if she were forty years younger.

She had been told the colonel was a single man with a fascinating background. She showed no interest in Lenny or Jock. "They are not of the right background," she told a friend. She believed the colonel was a genuine retired military man and although, older than her usual 'targets' he was worth a try. She would do her best to interest him.

While she began her campaign, rehearsals were over for the day and Jock was sitting with members of the rock band, Guy and the Gorillas in the Coach and Horses. He told how suspended Detective Bamber had been harassing him, Lenny and the colonel, to confess they were still robbing banks and wouldn't believe Reg had died. "Arrested us, he did, took us to Croydon then had Reg's body exhumed and wouldn't believe the DNA. He says he's going to prove we raided those banks and post offices. He seems to think we rob the banks and hand the cash over to those that control us. Mad he is." This was a rare conversation where his speech was understandable, with a Glaswegian accent.

Retired judge, Carrington-Worth said nothing, he listened intently. John Watson, the retired banker and the bands drummer commented, "We told him you were with us when the banks and post offices were robbed."

Jock continued, "Well, he doesn't believe us."

Retired conservative cabinet minister and double bass player, Sir George Carter, asked if everyone wanted a refill and headed for the bar. Jock nodded acceptance for a whisky refill as the colonel and Lenny arrived.

The judge stood up. "What you two drinking, I'll get George to add them to the order."

He smiled and said, "It's good to see the phantom bank robbers are keeping out of trouble."

"Lenny usually has a bitter, mine's a G&T," the colonel continued.

The colonel chuckled as he sat down. Lenny looked puzzled and asked, "What's a phantom bank robber?"

"Never mind, for now, I'll tell yer later."

Lenny turned to Jock, "What's a phantom robber, Jock?"

"Just in someone's imagination."

Lenny continued to look baffled as a barman arrived with a tray full of drinks.

The judge was about to sit down when he patted the colonel on the shoulder and said quietly, "Don't worry, I'll have words in the right ears."

"Thanks, we've had nothin' do wiv these robberies. It's a bit comical really, they've got away wiv more cash than we ever did and the cops haven't got anywhere near catchin' 'em'."

They sipped their drinks in silence for a few minutes then began discussing how their stage acts could be improved.

155

After 20 minutes, the Trio left the band and headed home. The colonel managed to get to his flat without being spotted by Cynthia. An impatient Minnie was waiting for him when he entered his flat.

The colonel was feeding Minnie when he heard the TV news that at lunchtime a Bank in Balham, South London had been robbed by three old men wearing masks. One was described as having a ginger beard that finished half-way down his chest. Witnesses said the robbers had driven away in a red Mark 2 Jaguar. It was later discovered in a pub car park near Clapham Junction railway station. It had been stolen in Enfield the day before.

The police had no clues as to the identity of the gang. He smiled and said to himself, "Thank God, we were drinking with the judge and his band here in Bogwash at the same time."

In his countryside hideaway, Bamber saw the police mugshots of The Gang of Four, all taken less than six years, before he'd managed to get his sergeant at Croydon to send them to his mobile phone. He looked at his own picture of the man and believed it was Reg. He said out loud, "Plastic surgery. He's changed his appearance. Why did he catch a train to Southampton? I'll get me old pal with the Hampshire force to see if he knows him. That's the answer. Then I'll pick him up and interrogate 'im."

The next morning, the suspended detective drove to Southampton. He had no warrant card.

As he drove to the South coast port, the massive shape of 'Crackers' Crumb persuaded one of the elderly residents the Retreat to open the front door, so he could see his aunt who was deaf. As the door was opening, a slim elderly lady passed him pulling a suitcase on little wheels and headed for a taxi waiting at the main gate.

A neighbour told Crackers he'd just missed Joanna who'd gone on holiday. He failed to tell the fact to SOBS, who had employed him.

The spanking ladies of Brighton saw their business improve with Joanna's departure on holiday, they believed Crackers had frightened her away. They partly paid him in cash and two ladies together tied him to the bed and spanked his huge backside. The SOBS believed he had helped restore their business. All was peaceful on the chastisement front.

Lenny sat alone in The *Gripe and Groan* waiting for the colonel and Jock, he missed his speech lessons with Joanna, he had never been caned for getting things wrong.

In Southampton, Bamber was thwarted in his efforts to meet up with his old police college friend Inspector Iain Harness. He was away on his honeymoon with his second wife. As his visit was unofficial, he decided not to ask any other officer for help.

But all was not lost, he thought. As he sat in the car park near the station, he saw the man who he believed was a disguised Lenny get out of a blue Ford Mondeo and walk into the station. By the time Bamber entered the station and shouted, "Police, let me through." He waved a card with his picture on. The guard at the ticket barrier thought it was a warrant card and let him through in time to see the London-bound train departing. It was later discovered he'd quickly flashed his plastic driving licence contained in a black wallet with the Metropolitan Police Crest at the top, he'd handed over his warrant card, but not the wallet it was in, when he was suspended.

A frustrated Bamber drove out of Southampton with no clear idea where he was going. It was only midday. He decided he would have lunch near Salisbury on his way to his mum's and plan how to catch Reg.

He stopped near a bank, a rarity in a small town. He had a fear of using external cashpoint machines in case of robbery. He was queuing to use one of the machines housed in the main banking hall when three, apparently old, bearded men came in brandishing sawn-off shotguns and telling customers to lie down and not interfere.

Bamber tried to be the hero and said to the three gunmen, "I'm a police officer, put down your guns, you're under arrest."

The gunmen had masks covering their faces other than slit for their eyes and mouth. One, slightly taller than the others, had a ginger beard down to the middle of his chest. He stopped laughing when the bank's alarm went off and shutters came down across the door.

No money had been handed over when the bearded man ordered the bank staff to open the front door. He grabbed Bamber and said, "Do it, or he gets his head blown off, just do it." The bank staff complied and the three ran out of the bank empty handed. They forced Bamber out ahead of them and into the dark green Mark 2 Jaguar parked outside, its engine running. The bank's alarm bells were ringing as they drove off at speed.

The gang drove down a narrow country lane with Bamber sitting between two of the gang with a shotgun pressed against his throat. He tried to talk and was told to, "Shut it."

The driver in a Scots' accent, asked, "Okay, Chief, where do we drop him off?"

Around the corner, the driver stopped in a gateway to a field.

Bamber was dragged out of the car and told to take his jacket off, "Now take yer trousers off, yer pretend copper." Bamber, in fear of his life, complied. They threw his clothes into the backseat of the car.

One of the robbers took a length of rope from the front seat well of the car.

Now, wearing only his underpants he was marched to a nearby tree. They bound his wrists then tied him to a tree. They drove away at speed. Leaving Bamber struggling to get free. He started shouting for help.

Then his real fear emerged as a herd of Hereford bullocks, curious about the noise, surrounded him. A couple got close and sniffed him. He shouted at them to clear off. They shook their heads and stamped their feet, a couple snorted, giving him a smell of their fetid breath.

A tractor pulling a trailer with bales of hay on board and some full sacks, entered the field. The driver called for the animals to come and be fed. Surprisingly, they ignored him.

Ten minutes later, Bamber was free and the farmer called the police and an ambulance. A mile away, an elderly lady wondered why a perfectly good suit, shirt and shoes had been dumped in her dustbin. She also found Bamber's wallet.

Motor museums began locking out of sight any old Jaguars, particularly, Mark 2s and S-types. Some Mark 9s and 10s began to disappear from public view. Private owners were advised by the police to keep their prized vintage cars locked away out of view.

Bamber was furious when told the four who kidnapped him couldn't have been the colonel, Lenny and Jock along with the ghost of Reg. He believed the ginger beard of one man was part of the disguise, he ignored the fact that the original Gang of Four was beardless.

Chapter 34

THIS Friday night was a special entertainment night at the Retreat, this event masqueraded as a 'cabaret'. The entertainment was a ventriloquist. The replacement was Luke Lucifer and his little demon puppet along with a dummy black cat sitting on his right shoulder and a multi-coloured parrot with cross-eyes and misshapen beak on his left shoulder. Lucifer wasn't one of the best ventriloquist in the business, he and his three 'stooges' all suffered from a distinctive lisp.

The Trio had broken one of their social rules and attended the entertainment night. The three sat in the third row of chairs with the only vacant seat to the right of the colonel. To his dismay, Cynthia sat down next to him dressed in what she thought was her most alluring outfit. The colonel spotted that she was wearing a bra that accentuated her ample bosom and its lavender lace trimmings. She smiled sweetly at him between bright red lipstick she must have applied without the aid of a mirror.

He was further alarmed when she placed her hand on his knee as she said hello.

Lucifer began his act, he told a couple of 'jokes', that didn't raise a titter. At this point, the dummy cat fell off his shoulder. The elderly laughed. One shouted, "That was a bit of a catastrophe." He battled on with the little demon and parrot dummy 'chatting to each other', both with a lisp.

The colonel again lifted Cynthia's hand off his knee without smiling.

Lucifer made light of the cat disappearing from his shoulder. Little Demon stuttered the answer with his distinctive lisp, "Bumth 'im off, I did, made him dithappear, I did." No one laughed.

Cynthia again squeezed the colonel's knee. Without ceremony, he lifted it up and pushed it away again.

Lenny leaned over and whispered to the colonel, "This is crap, bloody awful."

The colonel whispered back, "Let's head for the Gripe." They stood up and nodded to Jock, silently signalling him they were leaving.

Cynthia placed her hand on his forearm and quietly said, "Oh, don't go. I was going to suggest we had tea together in my room."

"We've got a previous appointment with a masseuse."

"Yeah," Lenny added, "We take it in turns, she gives us a discount for a bulk order."

Outside the colonel turned to Lenny and said, "When were you injected with a sense of humour serum?"

"Yer, what? What yer on about? What's serum?" He asked in a puzzled voice.

"Never mind I'll tell you later. I did enjoy the look on her face," he said as they entered the pub.

Chapter 35

HAROLD Pearson now had a new ten-year passport and his facial twitch had become more intense. Anne Pritchard was visiting the catering company to organise the details of the wedding feast. Meanwhile, Harold was standing at a travel agent's deciding whether to fly to Kingston, Jamaica from Gatwick or take a cruise ship from Southampton. The latter appealed to him. Little did he realise that one of Anne's friends had spotted him in the travel agent's.

Two days later, recovered from being kidnapped and tied to the tree, Bamber decided he would stake out the Southampton Railway Station in the hope the new-look Reg Crowther would make an appearance. His plans were delayed as he visited a bank in Guildford. He ducked behind a desk as three elderly looking men entered the banking hall, blew a hole in the ceiling and demanded cash. One of them told the customers to behave and no one would get hurt.

As the three ran out of the bank, Bamber looked out of the window and saw the three being driven away in a Ford Mondeo. He rang Bogshire police headquarters and demanded Granger, Smith and Mackenzie be arrested for armed robbery. He gave the number of a blue Mondeo getaway car.

Half-an-hour following the blagging, the Fire brigade was called to a car on fire. The number plates were false. A single bobby was sent to the Retreat, he soon established the Trio had left aboard a large coach bound for Leamington Spa earlier that morning along with the Tartanettes and four other elderly men. Warwickshire police soon established the Trio had arrived along with others at one of the town's concert halls.

Bamber went home, believing he'd finally nailed The Gang of Four. He burst into tears later that night, when his former sergeant at Croydon nick told him the car, believed to be the one used, had been found as a burnt-out wreck and the three he wanted arrested had travelled, by coach, to the Midlands with many others before the raid took place.

Despite this set back, Bamber was still sure the mystery man seen visiting the Trio and later spotted at Southampton railway station, getting out of a blue Mondeo, was Reg Crowther. He discovered Iain Harness would be on duty the next day. Armed with his 'snatch' photographs he drove to the port early the next day. By mid-day, an angry Bamber departed the city. He'd been told the mystery man was a well-established solicitor in South Hampshire. He'd always looked like the pictures taken of him. Harness had no idea why Bamber was so interested in Simon Sourness, a respected lawyer specialising in probate issues.

Bamber tried to kick his mother's cat. "Out of anger," he told her. He tried to make friends with the feline and suffered deep scratches down his cheek for his efforts. His mother told him he deserved it and refused to stem the bleeding.

Back at the Retreat, Harold Pearson was trying to explain why he was visiting a Bogwash travel agent. His right eye twitched violently. He quickly responded, "I was just looking for somewhere to go for our honeymoon. I've got a load of brochures in the car. It was going to be a surprise."

Anne wet her right forefinger then pressed it to about-to-be husband's lips. "Surprise me after we're wed, darling."

Harold left his fiancé's flat and he breathed a sigh of relief. The wedding was scheduled in two weeks' time, he had to begin his plan.

He caught the bus to Brighton and buying a one-way airline ticket from Gatwick to Florida. Was his plan, flawless as he had thought?

He queued at the Dabbs Airline ticket desk to get his ticket to Tampa in Florida. They wouldn't accept him. "This is a one-way request for ticket, sir. You must have a return," the attractive girl with a gentle American accent explained. "Also you haven't got an EVTA."

"A what?" He asked.

The girl looked at him patiently. "An Electronic Visa Travel Authorisation." She smiled and went to the next passenger waiting. He stood pondering the situation when a uniformed man with four white rings on the lower sleeve of his jacket and a woman with three white rings on her sleeve, appeared each carrying a large black briefcase and a holdall with the name **Dabbs Airline**, and underneath, in script, the slogan, *The height of the best*.

As the two waited for a security gate to be opened, Harold Pearson decided to seek help to what he saw as his travelling dilemma. He would try the airport's information centre.

An hour later, he was boarding a train bound for Brighton and home, he'd discovered no EVTA, no travel.

Chapter 36

THE social flat once let to Walter Windsor had now been re-vamped and simply furnished. The council had hoped they had found the ideal female tenant.

Gloria Gainer told no one of her past. The Housing Department refuses to reveal how she qualified for a flat in the Retreat. She moved into Windsor's old flat.

At first, she kept away from fellow tenants, but this wouldn't last.

Like any community housing, elderly, some fragile individuals there was a turnover of residents, some heading for hospital, some in care homes, others the graveyard. The Retreat was no different. Steven Holmes had been in the home for nearly ten years and was very independent and managed without any social support. Suddenly, the 75-year-old developed a form of Alzheimer's, at least his doctor said it was. He was moved to a full-time care home.

Two days later Mavis Musgrove aged 77, a very independent and active individual, fell down a flight of stairs and broke both her legs. She was due to spend time in hospital recovering.

All was quiet for another week. Life at the Retreat continued its normal chaotic way. Clive Casper was an energetic 82-year-old. No one knew of his secret assignations with another, unidentified fellow female tenant.

The temporary warden, covering for Stella, called on the intercom to see if long-term tenant Clive was alright. She got no reply. It was two hours before his flat was entered and he was found dead in bed. Doctors said he'd died of a heart attack. Gloria, aged 80, was seen to be very tearful at the news. No one knew why.

That evening the Trio were late back. They'd been enjoying an evening drinking session with some of the ladies of the Tartanettes and Guy and the Gorillas. They had no idea that Clive had died earlier.

They entered the building and saw that in the lounge an array of candles flickered. Through the glass door, they saw the back of a figure in a hooded dark cloak standing in front of a table on which stood a strange array of figures and symbols. It was like an altar. They could hear the black-clad figure intoning some strange chants.

The colonel pressed the panic button in the reception area which rang in Bogwash police station. The chanting continued.

The Trio watched the figure and heard the intonations. Two policemen arrived. Jock opened the door and before they could say anything he put his finger to his lips denoting silence. Another squad car pulled up in the road outside the Retreat. Jock went through the same, 'be quiet' routine with two lady constables and let them in.

The four representatives of Bogwash police could hear the chanting and noisily entered the lounge. The black-clad figure spun around and shouted, "How dare you interrupt my service, get out."

The colonel quietly said to one officer, "That's Miss Gainer, she lives in flat 12."

One constable asked her what she was doing.

"Ridding this place of malevolent forces. Someone in this building is destroying people's lives. They need to be dealt with. Now, go away you've angered my leader by interfering. Clear off."

One of the constables came forward, "Come with us, Miss Gainer, or should I say Verity Plummer."

The lady in the black cloak showed no emotion as she was escorted to the police car, two constables inspected her flat. They removed diaries and other mystic paraphernalia along with the strange alter in the lounge. They wouldn't tell the Trio or the temporary warden why she had been arrested.

In the morning, the colonel called Sergeant Wallace and was told he couldn't say why she had been detained. The warden had become secretive.

What lay behind the strange ritual and its secrecy bothered the colonel. He would ask the vicar what he understood what it was. He would have to wait. The Reverend Bernard Murphy, his wife Mary and the twins had gone to Nuneaton for a two-week break with his elderly parents.

Chapter 37

THE professor decided it was dangerous for him to continue *Teaching the wife the right way* and **Men, stand firm. Know your rights.**

He was unable to go anywhere without police bodyguard. He arrived at the *Gripe and Groan*, heavily disguised, along with his bodyguard.

He told the Trio he was going to cancel the two courses that were causing him so much trouble. The plain-clothes policeman muttered, "Thank God, we can live in peace."

The professor wouldn't tell anyone what his plan was. Tapping the side of his nose, he said, "I've thought of a winner."

Walking back to the Retreat, Lenny suddenly commented, "That professor fella is a right weirdo."

The colonel was quick to reply, "One recognises one, does one?"

'Ere, what?" Lenny asked.

A few days later, the Trio were enjoying their usual afternoon drink in the *Gripe and Groan* when a cheerful professor arrived without his bodyguard. He announced, "The demos have ceased, the women have gone away. I cancelled my courses. Peace." He bought himself a pint of lager and sat down with the Trio. "Creepology."

"What?" Lenny was quick to ask. Jock sipped his whisky and said nothing. The colonel took a mouthful of his beer from his nearly empty glass and leaned forward asking, "Say that again."

"'Creepology', the art of saying the right thing at the right time. It's an art form few people can achieve successfully. I plan on producing a course leading to a degree. Just what a man or woman needs to give themselves a better life."

The Trio looked at each other, the colonel pushed his empty glass forward and said, "Professor, if yer fill the glass we'll listen to your latest plans." He smiled.

After buying a round of drinks the professor expanded on his plans. "The course will be ideal for Members of Parliament, locally elected councillors and officials. Other groups include radio, TV and newspaper journalist, bank managers, salesmen, both on-line and door-to-door will be course targets.

"All these groups presently practice being creeps with various degrees of success. I want to see that the art is delivered professionally, with the possibility of a University degree acknowledging this."

Lenny was the first to respond, "Cor, does this mean I could stand a better chance with totty. Yer know, give them the right chat-up line?"

Jock burst out laughing and said in his best understandable English, "Lenny, it would need more than a training course to make you an articulate creep."

Lenny sat back with a confused, then a hurt look on his face.

The professor enthusiastically added, "I'm still working on the finer points of the prospectus. I believe I've devised a winner. The idea is to make anyone completing the course be skilled at smarminess. The course will also give someone the qualification of a creepologist."

"What the 'ell is one of them?" Lenny demanded.

"The study of the history of being a creep. How did it originate, the various styles, etcetera, a complete study. I think it will be a good tool to help cool down frustrations and to make the world a calmer place to be."

The professor sat back and smiled at the Trio and turned the palms of his hands upwards as if looking for acceptance.

The colonel picked up the sheet of A4 on which the Professor had outlined his plans; he read.

Prospectus

To be a successful creep you need to follow the following basic rules.

1. Do not show any signs of nervousness.
2. Avoid perspiring and sweaty palms.
3. Always look your target in the eyes. Do not look away.
4. It is important you demonstrate that you are relaxed.
5. Always smile, it gives the other side comfort.
6. At the beginning, do NOT tell women they are beautiful or the male handsome. Use phrases like, 'You look elegant' or if addressing a male, "You look so confident, I like confidence in a man." Say it if you mean it, even if you don't.

7. Do not smoke in front of your target, or offer them a cigarette, they may not smoke.
8. Only buy soft drinks.

The colonel smiled and put the sheet back on the table. "Nothing new with this," he commented.

"Oh, this just a list of ideas, I've got more to add," the professor replied with a chuckle. "I'll be just right on the night, this is just a draft."

"How do you manage now, with that Worthy woman," the colonel asked.

"She keeps out of my way. Has her own followers."

Chapter 38

FOR the Trio, it was nearly a year and a half at the Retreat; the last six months on a two-year suspended sentence following their farcical attempt to rob a closed down post office in Bogwash. They were beginning to get used to the world outside various prison cells. The colonel worked on his after dinner speaking engagements and his planned book on his life as a failed bank robber. Lenny began enjoying his role as a driver for the Tartanettes. Jock worked hard on his new life as part of a show business dressed as a highlander and displaying his skills with a set of bagpipes.

When sober, he spoke in a strange language he said was Gaelic. No one could understand a word he'd uttered. This had frustrated many police forces and prosecution lawyers when caught. Courts usually nodded as if understanding his verbal delivery of why he shouldn't be jailed. He usually was, with a recommendation; he learned decipherable English.

Scotland Yard detectives discovered a solution. Half a bottle of whisky before interrogating him. The Highland Spirit had a strange effect on his speaking style. He forgot to speak in the strange language he claimed was pure Scottish, or as he frequently said, 'Ecosse'.

He appeared to enjoy confusing anyone he was unsure of. Such a person was Professor Giles Galbraith who claimed in his tenancy application that he was a retired nuclear scientist and spoke many languages, he didn't disclose which ones. He'd moved into the private wing of the Retreat and in the early days of his tenancy he was rarely seen at any social gatherings or visits to the lounge.

In his visits to the lounge, he would sit silently and listen to the chatter around him, stroking his Van Dyke style greying goatee beard or twiddling the ends of his handle bar moustache.

The colonel was determined to discover the secret world of the man who called himself professor. He asked Sergeant Wallace if he knew anything about him. Three days later, the colonel was told his background was protected under a court order or something similar and he couldn't get anything further. An e-mail from an obscure government department told him to communicate with a Major Franks for a briefing. Sergeant Wallace was told in an e-mail Franks would, "Get back to him in a few days as he was out of the country." Jock spoke to him in his strange 'language'. All went quiet on the Professor Giles Galbraith front.

Joanna had a new client; he arrived for his first visit wearing a heavy herringbone overcoat with the collar turned up and a large bush-hat Australian-style. Although well-spoken he muddled up many phrases and willingly received her rear-end punishment. He left and told her he was very pleased with his lesson and would do his best to get phrases right the next time. No one recognised him when he departed.

On the following Sunday, she was half-listening and sometimes glancing at the TV programme, Parliament

Speaks, the announcer introduced Lord Cecil Cushing, the Government Minister for Social Correctness, part of his briefing was to reduce the number of unlicensed brothels and 'punishments' establishment. He calmly told the reporter, "We will licence the operations and take an annual fee, they will also have to pay tax like any other business, the Inland Revenue are working with us on this matter."

The reporter, without a glimmer of humour said, "Is it correct to say you are seeking to legalise these establishments for anyone to use?"

"Absolutely," he answered with a smile and walked away from the interviewer.

Joanna clapped her hands and laughed, "What? The dodgy old blighter, wait till he visits me again."

The colonel was thinking up some new stories about his life in the criminal underworld. Jock was playing his bagpipes in the wood. There were signs of an audience, cows or sheep. Lenny was in The *Gripe and Groan* waiting for the other two. He thought he would try his improved verbal delivery on two attractive teenagers who were sitting at the bar. The exchange was short and sharp, with one girl saying, "Clear off yer silly old beggar, go and catch a granny."

A despondent Lenny sat at a window seat and waited for his two pals.

The professor left the Retreat carrying a small brown suitcase.

As he was leaving Sergeant Wallace entered the *Gripe & Groan* ordered himself and the Trio a round of drinks. After the preliminary checks that everyone was in good health he asked, "Do you remember that woman Gainer whose real name was Verity Plummer, who was arrested doing some black magic stuff?"

"Yeees," the colonel slowly asked, "What about her?"

"Female con merchant, she's been returned to Manchester where she was wanted for connin' some elderly folk out of their savings. She's in court this morning. It seems she used this black magic ploy to scare the wits out of the vulnerable and then charge them a fee for exorcisms. Whilst she was organised, the rituals an accomplice would enter the old folk's flats and nick valuables. She was plannin' on doin' just that in the Retreat."

Lenny was the first to comment, "Wouldn't 'ave had much luck in my place, ain't got much worth nickin."

"Oh, I 'spect they'll give her slap on the wrist and a suspended sentence," the colonel added.

Chapter 39

IN Bogwash Park the 'professor' Galbraith sat on a lakeside bench and opened his little suitcase and soon had a collection of ducks, swans, pigeons and a couple of squirrels surrounding him taking advantage of the morsels of food he threw at them. After a while, he stood up and began to head back to the Retreat as police cars, fire engines and ambulances speedily and noisily headed for another part of town.

Arriving at the *Gripe and Groan* and planning to take their drinks outside and enjoying the afternoon sun, the colonel and Jock watched the activity as they entered the pub to find a miserable looking Lenny. "What ails thee, lad?" Jock asked as the colonel stood at one end of the bar and ordered their usual beverages.

Lenny gestured to the two young girls sitting at the bar giggling, with one of them displaying a great deal of upper thigh. "Them's two, said I, should grab a granny and leave them alone, the suggested, yer know, I wuz too old. Cheeky young buggers."

Jock chuckled saying, "Well yer ain't exactly youthful."

The colonel arrived, limping, as the barman with the drinks as another police car noisily sped past on the way to the town centre. He complained about his in-grown toenail saying, "Hospital in a couple of days to get this toe sorted. Can't have alcohol. They're keeping me in overnight 'cos of me age."

"We'll see yer in the afternoon," Lenny offered. Trying to be cheerful following his failed chatting up the totty episode.

In town, the police and emergency services wondered why someone would let off a series of thunder flashes attached to lamp posts. There was no real damage or casualties. As the police went about their business, Ricky Richmond climbed onto the canopy over the front door of the Job Centre. The outer two corners were supported by two Gothic-style uprights. Ricky was well-known to the police and welfare groups, all had tried to persuade him to take up the offer of sheltered accommodation. He consistently refused. The police often took pity on him when the weather was bad and took him into custody overnight for vagrancy, releasing him the next morning without charge.

He would tell the custody sergeant how pleasant the cooked breakfast was before they let him go. Ricky was always polite. The police delighted in 'banging-up' violent drunks in the same cell. They regarded the odour of the cell was part of the thug's 'punishment'.

Ricky had become adept at climbing onto the flat roof of the canopy. He said it avoided idiotic drunks and dogs urinating on him whilst he slept. The colonel had often seen him street begging and would drop any change he had into Ricky's battered old hat.

On the afternoon before the colonel was due to have his operation, another spate of explosions occurred in town. Ricky was still deciding if he would get up, climb down from his eyrie and start his begging activities. To any casual passerby, there was no sign that anyone was on the top of the canopy.

The two Doric-style pillars looked as if they were solid Portland stone. They were hollow plastic, simply supporting a lightweight canopy.

Another spate of thunder-flash style explosions occurred; two were attached to the Doric pillars. The canopy collapsed when the plastic melted, and Ricky's weight was too much for the canopy. It collapsed, tossing Ricky onto the pavement. He broke both legs and was taken to Bogwash hospital.

He lay in bed, his legs held up. He'd been cleaned up and was odour free. He'd even been given a shave and a haircut. He was unrecognisable to anyone who knew him as the towns' beggar.

Bogwash police were baffled by the series of explosions, who was doing it and why?

The Bugle ran a story of the mystery thunder flash explosions, the collapse of the canopy outside the Job Centre and one person injured. A short piece next to the main story told how the single injury was the town's well-known vagrant, Ricky Richmond.

MYSTERY
BOMBING
BAFFLES
POLICE

A series of explosions in the centre of town has left police searching for clues.

One person was injured when the canopy outside the Job Centre collapsed after support pillars caught fire.

The story went onto appeal for witnesses. The second story was more human-interest style.

VAGRANT
INJURED
BY BOMB

Local Vagrant Ricky Richmond was badly injured when the canopy on which he slept collapsed following a mystery explosion.

Police say he sustained serious injuries to his legs and pelvis in the fall.

A Bogwash hospital spokesman said he was doing as well as possible.

What they failed to say was the hours they spent washing and making him odour free before they could operate.

The story went onto tell how he had arrived in town some years before and had refused any offers of social help. The Bugle called for donations to help him in his recovery.

The residents of the Retreat were amazed when he was offered a furnished flat on the ground floor, with the rent paid out of social funds, when he was discharged from hospital.

His tenancy lasted a few days after tenants complained that he'd set up a pitch for his begging outside the Retreat. When anyone refused to give him a gratuity, he delivered a foul mouth lecture about their duty to help the oppressed and disadvantaged.

His parents arrived from Winchester to take him to their ten-bedroom mansion on the outskirts of the city.

Chapter 40

THE colonel was determined to go straight and worked hard on his memoires of his failed past. He urged the other two to follow his example.

Lenny had settled into the role of self-styled 'transport manager' for the Tartanattes. Jock had become better at his bagpipe and piano accordion playing and practiced in front of his regular audience, the herd of Ayrshire cows grazing in the field next to the wood, or on fellow residents, this usually followed the consumption of a large amount of whisky. His ability to speak in an understandable form of English, or what he described as educated Glaswegian, invariably followed. Most who knew him commented that his use of a weird language was diminishing, and he could be understood much more.

He'd spent the morning with the Tartanettes along with Guy and the Gorillas and by the early afternoon, he'd already consumed a half-bottle of Teachers.

He was beginning to cope with Martha and her declarations of affection for him, particularly when wearing his kilt.

Andy MacPherson had only been a tenant for a couple of days in the social wing, he was talkative and very anti-

English. Common phrases of his were, 'Damned English' or 'Bloody English'. One long-term resident commented, "He doesn't seem to like the English."

On this day, he'd accepted his first lift back to the Retreat in Martha's car. They walked into the lounge together to find there were many residents enjoying afternoon tea and cakes. Andy MacPherson was in full anti-English mode saying the Scots were better at making tea and cakes.

Jock put the case down containing his bagpipes and began his version of a well-known Scottish song in a reasonably good, understandable, Scots accent.

Should auld acquaintance be forgot
And ever brought to mind
Should wotsit doo-dah be tra-lah
Lah lah lah Ald lang syne
Lah-lah-lah thingummy boojit
Doo-dah doo-dah doo-dah-do
Dee-dum a cup o' kindness yet
For the sake of auld lang syne

When he'd finished many of the private and social wing residents politely clapped, even though they'd heard his version many times from him before. Jock took his bagpipes out of the case and began preparing to play them. He began playing his favourite, Scotland the Brave. His effort was shouted down by MacPherson, "Rubbish, damned rubbish, bloody Englishman wearing a kilt and playing a Scots tune, not on."

Jock put his bagpipes down and stared at MacPherson, Then, said in his version of Gaelic, "Cuach ye crio."

At which MacPherson responded, "And what sort of gibberish is that?"

Jock answered in English with a clear Scots accent, "You say you're Scottish, then you should know Gaelic. I'm not English, never have been and never will be. Scots born and bred, what aboot yersel?"

Jock held out his bagpipes and said, "If ye think ye can do better, let's hear it."

A voice at the back of the room shouted, "C'mon motor mouth, let's hear your effort. At least Jock does his best."

Martha had been standing nearby when she intervened saying, "Well, can you play the pipes? At least Jock does it for a living, very successfully."

Chapter 41

JOCK had travelled to Edinburgh to buy more flamboyant highland regalia to wear as his stage outfit when on stage with the Tartanettes and the Gorillas, he would spend some time with his daughter and be away for a few days. He told her he needed, "A wee bit of respite from the attentions of Martha."

The colonel was enjoying a quiet morning tidying and cleaning his flat; his peaceful domestic time was due to be disrupted.

The daily routine of the Retreat was remarkably without problems. That was until another temporary warden arrived. Clarise Clumber was one of the council's long-term warden's and normally took over duties if one left or went on leave. She was a stickler for rules. One of these was her anti-pet stance, even for someone keeping a goldfish in a bowl. She decided that she would undertake a snap inspection of some tenants suspected of keeping pets. She had a tip-off that a cat was often seen climbing through a window of the colonel's flat. She decided to act and have him kicked out for disobeying the 'No pets' tenancy agreement.

The colonel had paused his housekeeping and decided to make a cup of tea. Suddenly, Minnie let out a long meow fled from the chair and jumped out of the window and climbed down the oak tree. A puzzled colonel stood and watched Minnie leave. He was stirring the tea when suddenly the door was opened and Clarise Clumber, along with two uniformed council security guards entered, without knocking. "Right, stay where you are," she shouted and turned to the two unsmiling men. "Right, search the place," she turned to the colonel and said, "Okay, make it easy fer yer self and tell us where the moggy is."

The colonel kept his composure and asked, "Moggy, what moggy is that?"

She glared at him, saying, "The black and white one that sits in your window." One guard up-turned the settee and the second opened the oven door.

"It would have been polite if you had knocked first," the colonel said quietly as he sipped from his mug of tea. He said, "The one sitting on the window sill in my bedroom?" Clarise, with one of the men, headed for the bedroom.

The colonel turned to one of the grim-faced security men and said, "Don't forget the loo, the moggy might be taking a bath."

The security man entered the bathroom, checked the batch, lifted the toilet sea to ensure the cat wasn't taking swimming lessons. He tipped the contents of the dirty washing basket onto the floor looking for a cat. He walked out leaving the contents on the floor.

Clarise returned holding a large black-and-white stuffed cat with a one glass eye, she put the toy down and glared at the colonel and without saying a word she left with the two unsmiling men.

The colonel was unaware his dirty laundry was now lying on the floor as the three left his flat.

He peered out of the window and saw the three leave the building. He saw one of the men pointing to something along the road. The colonel looked to where the man was pointing and saw Minnie sitting on the roadside wall outside the neighbouring house. Clarise Clumber was to show her hatred of cats and with the two men tried to catch Minnie.

The colonel laughed at the outcome. One man stretched his hands out attempting to catch Minnie, he failed, and he fell to the ground clutching his face, Clarise was attempting to hold in place the front of her blouse, it had been torn away by Minnie, exposing her bra. The cat vanished from the scene.

Lenny was walking back home when two police cars and a paramedic drove past, sirens sounding and turned into the lane in front of the Retreat. An ambulance followed.

The paramedic was patching up scratches to one man's face and hands. A police constable was talking to Clarise who was giving him a dramatic version of events and trying to repair her ripped blouse and cover-up her exposed black lacey bra.

Lenny heard her shouting her demands that the 'criminal cat' be found and dealt with. The experienced constable was joined by a young female colleague. He was having difficulty keeping a straight face and replied, "Ma'am, we'll do all we can to arrest the miscreant and get him—"

"Or her—" The lady constable interrupted.

"Well, yes, and get 'em before the court," he continued.

Lenny went to his own flat, not having a clue about the existence of Minnie and amused that a cat could cause such mayhem.

The activity ended, and the colonel was chuckling as he took his empty tea mug to the kitchen, he washed it and returned to his lounge to find Minnie sitting on the armchair washing herself. He looked at her and said, "You certainly sorted out those two."

Minnie stopped washing, gave a long slow meow and began settling down on the chair. The colonel was convinced she had the equivalent of a feline smile on her face.

The colonel returned the one-eyed, stuffed black cat back on the bedroom windowsill, muttering, "Well, we certainly stuffed that Clumber woman."

Chapter 42

IT WAS now the spring and the bad winter had taken its toll on two of the elderly residents of the Retreat. They were now resting in the graveyard of St Jaspers.

Their vacant flats were soon cleared, re-decorated and were either sold or, in the social wing, let to the financially needy tenants. This was the case of the man called the 'Squire'. He wouldn't say why he was called this and no one else seemed to know.

He was a man of few words; when he did speak it was in a language no one understood. He would occasionally visit the lounge and sit quietly listening to the chatter of the other tenants.

The 'Squire', or to give him the name his tenancy was in, Donald Draper. No other information was available on his personal file held at the council offices. It simply showed his date of birth, indicating he was 79-years-old.

The Trio had never spoken to this strange man who dressed in green plus fours, tucked into thick green woollen socks and wore brown brogues. He had a matching hacking jacket in a similar pattern as his trousers. He set this sartorial look off with a deerstalker hat.

The three were returning from rehearsals with the Tartanettes when they decided to have a break to have a drink in the Waterman bar on the sea front. They'd only just downed it when the distinctive figure of the 'Squire' appeared. The barman asked what he wanted, he pointed at a pump on the bar saying it was a Fullers Best Bitter. He never said a word and sat down at a window seat.

Jock was the first to say anything. "He's weird, never speaks to anyone and when he does, it's a just a babble, and the way he dresses is summit else."

The colonel laughed. "You should know about verbal babble. I thought you were the expert."

Jock said nothing.

Back at the Retreat, two police cars and four officers were attempting to persuade Brenda Bates to leave her flat and go with them to the police station. A paramedic was tending to the head wound of Bertie Bemrose, a long-time tenant who had never caused any problems. Witnesses say he'd tried to get out of way as she staggered along the corridor, frequently taking a gulp from a nearly empty bottle of Haig whisky. He'd tried to dodge her as she swayed in front of him. He made the mistake of telling her she was drunk. She took another gulp of whisky and hit him over the head with the empty bottle shouting as she did so.

The Trio arrived back in time to see an ambulance, blue lights flashing, siren sounding leaving the area, soon followed by a police car with Brenda in the back seat.

As the three were about to enter the building, Lenny saw the 'Squire' in the distance. He'd seen the police car ducked out of sight behind a tree. "That's queer," Lenny said.

"What's queer?" the colonel asked.

"That Squire fella has just dodged outa sight when he saw the cops," Lenny replied.

The police cars left the area and the Squire appeared from his hiding place, looked around and headed for the Retreat. He smiled at the Trio but said nothing; he let himself in through the street door which closed behind him.

The three looked at him, stared at each other and shrugged their shoulders, bewildered at his actions.

Lenny was the first to say anything. "Got summit to hide that fella has."

"Maybe," the colonel responded as the street door opened and they walked in.

Minnie watched the Trio from the behind the branches of the Oak tree then jumped onto the balcony of the colonel's flat and through the small gap of the open window.

Chapter 43

ON THE train, returning from a two-day visit to London, Belinda smiled at the information she now had. But, what could she do about it. She knew about Styles, but what was she going to do about Donald Draper? The man who called himself 'Squire'. She already knew that if asked about himself, he answered in a strange language and purported not to understand anyone who spoke to him. She hoped old friends could help her solve the mystery.

The colonel looked out of the window of his flat and saw Lenny heading for the bus stop to catch the service into town. The colonel mused, "I wonder where he goes at this time every Saturday?" He muttered. Then he saw the 'Squire' leaving. "I'd like to know more about him."

Minnie let out a meow, her lips quivering as she re-positioned herself on the chair and went back to sleep.

"Okay, you rest," the colonel told Minnie as he put his jacket on. "I'm going for a pint." Minnie's tail twitched. The colonel headed for The *Gripe and Groan* where he knew Lenny and Jock would eventually turn-up.

He was surprised to see the 'Squire' sitting alone in the corner of the bar holding a pint of bitter. The colonel ignored him and watched him from the other end of the bar and saw him reading a copy of that day's *Mirror* newspaper.

He thought, "Mmm, can't speak understandable English, but he reads a red-top English newspaper. Very interesting." As he mulled this over, the 'Squire' got up, pushed the 'paper' in his pocket and left the pub. It was now late afternoon and Lenny and Jock passed the 'Squire' as they entered the building. He ignored them.

The colonel bought Lenny a pint of lager and Jock his usual 'wee dram'. As they began enjoying their drink together, the colonel said, "Jock, your linguistic talents are understandable in comparison with that 'Squire fella'."

Jock smiled and sipped his whisky.

They'd been sitting and chatting when Belinda appeared and joined them. The colonel offered to buy her a drink. She chose a tonic water with a little ice, Lenny went to the bar and bought a fresh round of drinks.

As he waited at the bar she commented that she had just seen the mystery man, the 'Squire'.

The colonel said he had been in the pub reading a daily newspaper. "There's something odd about him, just like that Professor Galbraith fella," he commented.

"Doesn't say much and when he does, it don't make sense. I fink he's a foreigner who can't speak our lingo," Lenny announced and sat back with a triumphant look on his face.

Belinda said nothing.

As the four walked back to the Retreat, a red-faced, well-dressed man, wearing a trilby, walked past with a smile on his face and opened the driving door of the top-of-the-range Jaguar and rubbed his posterior. None of the four commented.

Joanna sat and drank a small sherry and decided she would have to limit the number of her clients as it was tiring her. She wondered why so many, apparently well-spoken men wanted English-language lessons and were willing to receive a caning if they got it wrong. Very strange.

As the four were entering the lounge Henry Styles was counting out a bundle of notes. Another two bundles lay to one side. Three elderly ladies watched him.

Belinda grabbed the colonel's arm and said, "Stick by me, I've got to put a stop to this."

She walked over to the three elderly ladies and then to the man known as Styles and said, "Still up to your old tricks, Sampson, or should I say Smith, Sloman or Singer. Aren't they some of your aliases when you've fleeced elderly people out of their savings? Now, give the ladies their money back and you won't get arrested for theft, just attempting."

He grabbed the other two bundles of money and shouted, "Get outa my way." As he went to leave, he was stopped when the colonel tripped him up with the aid of his walking stick, falling to the floor, he dropped the money from his hand.

"Going somewhere?" The colonel shouted, "Not anymore, you are not."

Lenny grabbed the cash before it flew away.

The age-old theory that a policeman could never be found when they were wanted, was about to blown out of the window as four constables walked through the front door. The two men and two women team had arrived to give residents a talk on Spotting Confidence Tricksters. A phone call confirmed Styles was wanted by Thames Valley police, under the name of Sloman, after robbing pensioners of their savings in Oxford.

The next morning, the colonel was looking out of his lounge window and saw Donald Draper walking up the road. He muttered to himself, "There's something not right about that man."

It was to be months before the mystery was solved.

Chapter 44

THE colonel received a letter from Angela saying she and her son were planning to return to the UK. She didn't give a date. He remembered that British doctors had said James suffered from autism. America doctors claimed it was a strange illness called Pandas Syndrome. The librarian helped the colonel find details on the internet. He read details of the illness.

'Streptococcus pyogenes (stained red), a common group: A streptococcal bacterium. PANDAS is hypothesised to be an **autoimmune condition** in which the body's own antibodies to streptococci attack the basal ganglion cells of the brain, by a concept known as molecular mimicry.

'Paediatric autoimmune neuropsychiatric disorders associated with streptococcal infections (PANDAS) is a hypothesis that there exists a subset of children with rapid onset of obsessive-compulsive disorder (OCD) or tic disorders and these symptoms are caused by group A beta-haemolytic streptococcal (GABHS) infections. The proposed link between infection and these disorders is that an initial autoimmune reaction to a GABHS infection produces antibodies that interfere with basal ganglia function, causing symptom exacerbations. It has been proposed that this autoimmune response can result in a broad range of neuropsychiatric symptoms.

'The PANDAS hypothesis was based on observations in clinical case studies at the US National Institutes of Health and in subsequent clinical trials where children appeared to have dramatic and sudden OCD exacerbations and tic disorders following infections. There is supportive evidence for the link between *streptococcus* infection and onset in some cases of OCD and tics, but proof of causality has remained elusive. The PANDAS hypothesis is controversial; whether it is a distinct entity differing from other cases of Tourette syndrome (TS)/OCD is debated.

'PANDAS has not been validated as a disease entity; it is not listed as a diagnosis by the International Statistical Classification of Diseases and Related Health Problems (ICD) or the *Diagnostic and Statistical Manual of Mental Disorders* (DSM).'

The colonel closed the computer down and sighed. He was, to a large extent, confused with the medical terminology. What he recognised was that the boy had some sort of behavioural problem.

He returned to the Retreat and as he entered his flat, Minnie jumped down from the small open window and sat in front of her feeding bowl, with a look of expectation on his face.

After feeding him, he sat pondering what he'd understood of what he had read. Minnie joined him on the settee. "Well, old thing, I'm just as baffled as I was before, why can't these so-called experts communicate in plain, understandable, English?"

Chapter 45

ON the train journey to Southampton, to give a talk to a group of lawyers, the colonel thought he would tell his audience that armed bank and post offices were in decline despite the mystery of a gang emulating his old team.

He pondered who they could be and why? He reflected how pleased he was that the police had cleared the Trio from all involvement and the National Banker Robbers Federation and had declared that none of their members were involved.

He considered the implications of the news that the Federation were planning on winding-up their activities as membership had declined and revenues from membership fees had dropped dramatically over the previous twenty years along with the percentage of the take each gang had to pay the Federation from a successful heist.

The Federation sent members a newsletter telling them of the decline in the industry. As the train sped along, he read the statistics from 1992 when Federation members were involved in more than 800 blagging. He raised his eyebrows when he read that this number had dropped to 50 in twenty-five years. He muttered to himself, "Better security screens and more CCTV, we didn't stand a chance. The end of an era. Oh, well."

A lady sitting opposite looked at him with a puzzled expression. The colonel smiled at her as he left then train at Southampton. His talk was virtually a repeat of the one he had delivered in Bristol. It resulted in a similar audience response.

On the train back home, he reflected on the number of strange tenants at the Retreat, some very suspicious. He arrived back at Bogwash and decided he would take his briefcase home before joining Jock and Lenny for an evening drink. He was about to leave home when his telephone rang. To his surprise, it was Tommy Gunn of the Federation asking if he could meet him and he was prepared to come to Bogwash the next day. They arranged to meet in the lounge bar of the *Gripe & Groan* at midday.

It was four o'clock when he arrived at the pub. For ten minutes, he told Jock and Lenny of his lunchtime talk when Sergeant Wallace appeared and sat down with them after buying a pint. He told them of a new team, led by the Met, formed to track down the mystery four. He told them they were under considerable political pressure to find the culprits. He added that the Home Secretary and the Commissioner of the Met were to give a joint press conference at five o'clock and it would be shown live on the main TV channels and heard on the radio.

The Trio and the Sergeant moved to another part of the pub to see the broadcast on a wide screen TV. On time the BBC news picked up the transmission of an outside broadcast crew outside New Scotland Yard. With the rotating sign in the background, a stern looking Home Secretary, Sir Gerald Good fellow faced the camera with the Commissioner, Sir Peter Planter, with the peak of his cap pulled down over his eyes. Sir Gerald began reading from a sheet of paper. Lenny yawned.

Sir Gerald began, "A gang of bank robbers are raiding smaller banks and local post offices the government are urging all police forces to share information and will make ten-million-pound fund available as extra resource to catch these felons before they kill someone. I will now hand you over to the Commissioner Sir Peter Planter." He turned and gestured to Sir Peter, who began reading from his pre-prepared statement. He looked down, the peak of his cap obscuring the top of his face.

"We are putting all our resources into catching this gang and are grateful to the Home Secretary for providing extra central government funding in order to catch them. We have already eliminated a number of suspects and have been given a great deal of help from the criminal underworld."

With that, he and the Home Secretary turned around, and headed for the comfort of the Yard's offices, leaving the press shouting questions at their backs without a response.

There was a few minutes silence as Lenny yawned and Jock headed for the bar to order another round. The colonel leaned forward and said to Wallace, "At least we're being believed."

Suddenly, the local news channel presenter told of a bank robbery in Guildford in which a gang of four old men raided a bank and escaped with £20,000 and escaped in a stolen vintage Jaguar car.

That night, four men sat in an Oxford pub and laughed at the ten o'clock national news and the coverage of the Home Secretary and police commissioner's 'conference'. There was no mention of the Guildford bank raid.

Lenny commented that Celia Worthy or members of class didn't use the *Gripe* anymore. He wondered why.

No one offered an answer.

Jock and Lenny decided they need provisions from the convenience store, whilst the colonel headed home. As he was about to enter the street door, he noticed Minnie's tail disappear though the open window to his flat.

Chapter 46

BOGWASH police received a copy e-mail from Boggy Moor prison that had been distributed to all police forces saying Rastafarian drug grower and dealer Sonny Summerton had absconded from an outside working party and may turn up in Bogwash. They sent a current picture of him without his distinctive dreadlocks. He was easily identified because of his facial skin being blotchy white with black streaks, all thanks to the plastic surgery after the green house explosion at the Retreat.

Sergeant Wallace met the Trio in the *Gripe and Groan* that evening and told him Summerton had escaped and he may head for Bogwash as he had threatened revenge on those who had caused the explosion that had ruined his, self-stated, film star good looks and his crop of cannabis.

Lenny looked at the picture and said, "With a face like that it must be easy to know who he is and catch 'im."

The colonel added, "When I doused that crop with petrol, I didn't expect him to light a fag, throw the match away and blow the place up."

The Sergeant said, "Let's have another drink. All you have to do is watch your back. You've got my numbers if you see anything suspicion." He looked at the colonel and added,

"You've now got a mobile, keep it with you and use it if you have to."

The Sergeant bought the Trio a round of drinks and when finished, he left them. He said on departing, "My wife's more important than you three, goodnight."

The three made their way back to the Retreat. The colonel found his 'lodger' fast asleep and in no hurry to be fed and watered.

Two days later, at six in the morning the colonel was gazing out of the corridor window looking over the rear garden and the blackened remains of the greenhouse. He saw a figure slowly and furtively walking towards the rear entrance of the garage. Dressed in a long raincoat and his head covered by a woollen hat, he entered the building. The colonel called Sergeant Wallace. He was surprised to see two uniformed constables run towards the rear entrance. What happened next could have been written by a comedy writer.

The colonel saw them fiddle with the door then run back to the front of the side of the building. A police car arrived, and two more constables joined them and hid from view of the side window. It opened and a spade, fork and a set of shears came hurtling out. Coming out backwards, came the figure of the man with the long coat and woollen hat, he slipped and began to fall, suddenly suspended half-way out as his coat became snagged on the window latch.

The colonel could see and hear the sequence of events from his flat window. The four constables surrounded him. He was an all-black faced guy. One of the constables said, "Sonny, I presume?"

The man shouted back in a distinctive Caribbean accent, "Let me go you thugs, I ain't Sonny." He struggled to free himself as his coat began to rip, one of the constable pulled the hat off his head whilst another picked up a hosepipe and washed the man's face with a jet of cold water. The black boot polish was washed away exposing the very blotchy face and short-cropped hair of Sonny Summerton. His coat gave way and he fell to the floor and was handcuffed.

The colonel later learned, he'd been returned to a high security prison in the North of England.

Chapter 47

IT was midday as Jock serenaded a herd of young heifers in a wood alongside a field on the outskirts of Bogwash. Lenny was running errands for the Tartanettes. The colonel waited in the lounge bar for the arrival of Tommy.

He didn't realise how short the Chairman of the Federation was until he walked in with two burly, sunglass wearing, bodyguards. He looked up at the colonel and said, "Good to see you again. You two leave us alone." The two big men sat at the far end of the bar as Tommy hauled himself onto a bar-side stool and ordered a sparkling water with a slice of lemon and a straw.

"You look fine and well, living the non-activity of a retired old blagger. Gawd, your activities were legendary. Tell me, did you ever get to spend the money you nicked?"

The colonel looked at the floor and shook his head, "Always got caught, never free long enough to spend the take. Never spent a penny."

Tommy then began, "Now, let's get t'the business why I'm here. It's these bank raiders by four old geezers. Now it ain't you lot, is it? Sorta comin' outa retirement."

The colonel laughed. "There's only three of us now, when some of these raids were underway we were some miles away with rock solid alibis."

The diminutive top gangster, his feet dangling a few inches above the floor and sucking some sparkling water through the straw said, "We wuz plannin' on closin' down the Federation until this spate of robberies by some old geezers. They even nicked cars like the ones you used't."

Tommy went quiet, swinging his feet backwards and forwards, and gazed into the distance before he carried on, bowing his head, "We needs your 'elp to catch these blighters. The Federation 'as voted to give the cops maximum help."

The colonel stroked his moustache and slowly asked, "You're teamin' up wiv the cops to catch these blaggers?"

"Too true, these guys are givin' decent, hardworkin' villains a bad name, they've gotta be caught. Yer wouldn't believe the grief us professionals are bein' given, just 'cos of those nutters. Don't even belonging to our Federation, they've got no idea that if they pay's their fees and gives us a cut of any take from a heist the we look after members in their retirement. Well, I mean yous and yer team get our benefits. We don't call it a pension, just a retirement grant. I wouldn't worry, if I were you, we've got plenty of dosh in the kitty, however, if we find's out anyone in the Federation is backin' 'em then we'll suspend, probably even stop, their benefits." He took another drag of water through his straw and gave the colonel a meaningful look.

"That's comforting," the colonel quietly replied. "Now, what can I do to help?"

Tommy put his glass down on the bar and continued. "Just reassure me you've nuthin' do wiv these scum who are givin' genuine blaggers a bad name."

The colonel straightened his back and stroked his moustache. "You've no idea what the three of us do now. Let me tell you. We all earn an honest, crime free, existence. It's important we follow the letter of the law and keep free of any crime. Jock plays the bagpipes as part of a theatrical group, Lenny drives them around in a mini-bus. I spend my time giving talks about my days as a blagger and write my memoires. As, I said, we lead an honest life. This has been the longest period we haven't been banged up, just beginn' to enjoy our time out of chokey. Not in our best interest to be involved. Anyway, we'll help yer all we can."

Tommy smiled, and sipped more water. "No offense meant, we have to maintain our standards, even though we're closin' down. We're prepared to give the cops as much 'elp as we can, just to show professional blaggers are quite decent really. Where's the barman, I need another water. What's your tipple?" Tommy then called over the two heavy weight minders, each standing more that six-foot tall and weighing some 110 kilos and introduced them to the legendary colonel.

Ten minutes later, Tommy left with his two 'minders on each side of him. He thought how incongruous the sight of little villain and two large minders looked as they walked out of the pub.

He walked into the public bar to find Lenny and Jock had just bought a round of drinks. Unusually, Jock went to the bar to buy the colonel a drink. Neither of his two henchmen had seen him with Tommy or saw the 'Chairman' leave with his minders. The colonel chose to remain quiet about the meeting.

Chapter 48

MAIDSTONE wasn't a town he knew. He'd never blagged a bank or stood trial at the Crown Court. It was a Saturday and he was due to give a talk to lawyers and retired police officers. It was a rare day to be giving a talk. On the train journey, he pondered who the four mystery bank robbers were; why had the suspended Detective Bamber been quiet for so long? Why did Lenny disappear for several hours on a Saturday when not at rehearsals or a concert?

He was delighted to see the theatre was full. He was going to enjoy giving his talk. He forgot about Bamber and Lenny as he prepared to meet the audience.

In Swindon, Bamber walked alongside a row of shops still convinced the Gang of Four were 'still at it'. He was not assured Reg was dead. He took a break and had lunch in a town centre pub.

In an Indian restaurant in Bogwash, Lenny was enjoying his lunch with a female companion. He was trying hard to speak in an intelligible speech pattern and behave in a 'gentlemanly' manner. He'd found a woman he could talk to, and not behaving like a crude and foul-mouthed oaf.

Jock sat alone in the *Gripe and Groan* and downed his third large whisky just as Martha arrived looking for him and suggested they had a late lunch together. His consumption of whisky had mellowed him, and he was happy about walking, holding her hand to the Peking Palace.

In Maidstone, the colonel looked across at the faces of his audience and shuffled his papers. He began by clearing his throat. "The public at large have a general belief that armed robberies were carried by men. Not so, women can be just as adept at armed raids. This was the case of one lady, I won't name her, in case she sues."

The audience laughed.

"She first came to police attention when she single-handedly robbed a Harlow bank and escaped on a powerful motor bike. Soon after, she crashed it to avoid hitting a deer crossing the road. She served five years.

"The next time she appeared was as one of our students at Heist Away. She was now nearly sixty. She never did rob another bank, she became a social welfare administrator at the Federation of Bank Robbers looking after the families of banged-up robbers.

"The last I heard of her she had married a retired lawyer and was living in the South-West of England. It goes to show, being a heist merchant, can have its benefits."

There were loud guffaws from the audience and a loud voice shouted, "My wife robs me every day."

A female voice called out, "Good."

The colonel looked down at his notes, adjusted his spectacles and continued, "One of our, potentially, most successful heist was thwarted by a woman driver. We pulled up outside a bank in Guildford to do the business, then just as we entered the bank and do the business, a car pulled up behind our stolen Jag. Then reversing lights came on from a car in front of ours and the indicator started flashing. Alongside ours, a blue car pulled with four people in it waiting for the car in front of ours to move. Effectively, we were blocked in.

We ran out of the bank and into the Jag. We were blocked in and Jock gave a blast on the horn. Lenny suddenly said, "It's the cops." Two of the occupants of the blue car had got out and came around to the driving side. They were two uniformed offices. A woman wound down the driving window of the blue car, put on a hat with black and white chequered band and showed a warrant guard.

"Then the driver of the white car in front of us got out and flashed a warrant guard. We later discovered she was a Detective Inspector who was on her way to work. We had managed to nick twenty-six thousand from the bank. The best we'd ever achieved. Never got a chance to spend a penny of it. I blamed a female driver trying to leave a parking bay." He smiled as the audience began to jeer.

A female voice was heard shouting out, "Sexists."

Unfazed by the interruption, the colonel carried on, "Yes, we'd been thwarted more than once when a woman blocked our efforts. Let me tell you of one embarrassing incident in a Hounslow post office. Thanks to Reg's early stages of his illness, he was in hospital undergoing tests. It looked like a simple blaggin' so we decided to do it three handed. Jock was drivin' the nicked car, as usual. Lenny and I went in, he let off one barrel of the sawn-off just to scare people. I was at the counter telling the lady that I wanted the contents of the till. Lenny was behind me. The next thing I knew was I got a blow to the back of me head. As I fell the shotgun was snatched from me hand, then I saw Lenny lying on the floor with someone pointin' his shotgun at his head.

"The next thing I knew me wrists and ankles were tied together wiv those plastic tie fings. It was later that we discovered that me and Lenny had been clobbered by a seventy-five-year old pensioner, a retired army sergeant. Jock found himself looking down the barrel of a sawn-off being wielded by an off-duty woman police sergeant, the daughter of the old lady."

"I has t'tell yer we took a lot of stick from other inmates when we got banged up. It was, in fact, the only time we got sentenced without Reg. Who'd have thought an old lady and her daughter could have spoilt a blaggin' that should have been a push over.

"I'll finish on another tale where we were thwarted by a woman in our attempt, for the first time, to get away with a heist of a Bracknell Bank. We lifted twenty-two thousand. Later that night, we were havin' a quiet drink in a Streatham, South London pub, we hadn't yet split the money which was still in a holdall in the back of the car. Then outa the blue, a dozen or so gun-toting cops came directly to our table and we were nicked. No messin' about.

"We wuz baffled at first how we got caught. It seemed to us we'd pulled off a successful heist. What I will say is that Lenny never wore again the socks showin' characters from a Mickey Mouse movie. Jock has never used a particular brand of after-shave again.

"At our trial, it emerged that a young woman, was in the bank when we pulled of the blaggin. She'd given the cops a detailed description of what we were wearing. Later, she came to Streatham to see her mother and they were sittin' in the same pub as us.

"She phoned a Surrey detective who was investigatin' the raid. She described Lenny's socks and Jock's distinctive after-shave. He'd re-applied some on his face and gave his underarms a treat before we had arrived in the pub, hopin' he'd pull a bird fer the night. I understand the girl informant is now a full-fledged constable with the Surrey force."

The audience clapped and cheered as he gave a light bow and walked off the rostrum.

On his way home, he thought how his speaking events were becoming more successful. He began to reflect why Detective Bamber had gone so quiet and where did Lenny go when not looking after the transport needs of the Tartanettes. It was puzzling him.

He arrived back home, Minnie got up off the armchair, stretched and sat in front of the saucer which held his food and gave a quiet meow.

Bogwash police were still trying to identify the perpetrator of the thunder flash 'bomber' and why one vagrant was targeted along with harmless lamp posts.

Chapter 49

JOCK arrived at his woodland practice site to find there were no cattle in the neighbouring field to listen to his repertoire. Lenny was driving three of the Tartanettes on a shopping trip to Brighton. The colonel walked along the footpath of the River Boggy thinking about his meeting with Tommy Gunn and how they could catch the pretend Gang of Four and considering the content of his book and the story line of his next book, talk to the legal world. He was still wondering about Lenny's secret Saturday's.

At the Riverside pub, Harold Pearson sat alone sipping his second large whisky. His facial twitch had calmed down even though he was thinking about his forthcoming marriage to Anne Pritchard. He took a folded sheet of A4 paper out of his pocket and looked down at her suggestions of the guest list. None of the names were his relatives and friends. Despite this, he'd decided he would go ahead with the nuptials. No decision had been made regarding the honeymoon.

At the Retreat, Joanna read a letter suggesting she join SOBS and get the security benefits of the Society, for a fee, and asking for a meeting to discuss how their dispute could be amicably resolved. She contemplated the benefits of working with the Brighton 'professionals'. She had already stopped evening and weekend appointments, as too much spanking of stupid men was exacerbating the pain in her right arm.

As she sat and sipped a large sherry, she thought she might reduce the daily appointments to those she considered had greatly improved their English and only needed gentle chastisement.

In Twickenham, South London, a traffic warden started making out ticket after the driver of an S-Type Jaguar parked outside a bank stuck up two fingers to denote she should 'go way'. She continued making out the ticket as a gunshot was heard from within the bank. Seconds later, three masked, apparently old men, emerged from the bank, knocked her over, entered the car and sped away.

Three hours later, the colonel sat in his flat enjoying the tranquillity with Minnie and reading the Daily Mail, as his telephone rang. Tommy told him of the Twickenham raid and the Federation had escalated their support with the police in the hope of catching the rogue robbers.

Jock had arrived back at the Retreat and was preparing a meal when he heard the TV news tell of Twickenham bank raid. He shook his head at the news saying, "Who the 'ell are they?"

In Bogwash, Lenny was enjoying an Indian meal with a lady friend.

The colonel was looking out of his flat window and saw Donald Draper walking away from the Retreat looking furtively over his shoulder. "What is that man all about? I must ask Belinda if she had found more about him."

Some time had passed since Celia Worthy had been seen. The landlord of the *Gripe and Groan* commented to the Trio that the professor hadn't been seen for more than a week. Two of his students said he hadn't been seen at the University for the same time along with Mrs Worthy. The rumour mill began to work. Only to be demolished when told that the two hated each other.

Chapter 50

LATE in the morning as the bells of St Jaspers rang out, Harold Pearson sat in the right-hand front pew of the church with his best man alongside him. Cecil Cushing adjusted his thick horn-rimmed glasses and checked for the umpteenth time that the wedding ring was still in his pocket. Cecil had been the manager at the Bogwash branch of Buggins Bank for two months and had only met the groom on two occasions. Before retiring, Harold managed the bank.

He looked back at the entrance to the church and saw the left-hand side pews were full of Anne's friends. He saw her hairdresser, the lady from the fish and chip shop, the husband and wife who ran the weekly bingo sessions at the Retreat. No members of the Tartenettes were present, nor was Joanna Creswell. Behind him, the seats were empty. He wished he'd stood firm when he'd wanted to invite the Trio, but Anne refused to sanction their attendance. He felt a little lonely and was finding it difficult to smile and his left-hand side's facial twitch wouldn't stop.

He turned around to face the altar and found he was looking down at the Reverend Bernard Murphy checking his watch. He smiled and said reassuringly, "Don't worry, brides are allowed to be late, she'll be here soon." Beside him, Cecil

Cushing quietly hummed to himself. Secretly Harold hoped Anne had run away to avoid marriage.

Back at the Retreat, the Trio had gathered in the resident's lounge prior to heading for the *Gripe and Groan*. They were delayed when Anne appeared, along with another lady, and two young girls holding-up the train of her pink bridal gown. At the exit door, they stopped and arranged the veil across her face, then stepped out into the morning sunshine.

Seconds later, they were back, with Anne screaming and the others trying to calm her down and remove the veil from her head. The older woman then took the headgear and ran to the downstairs toilets. Lenny asked one of the weeping girls in charge of the train, what had happened. He reported his findings back to the others. "The girls say a naughty bird flew over and deposited its stomach contents on Anne's head."

The colonel and Jock stifled a laugh as the lady returned having cleaned up the veil. It was then replaced on her head. As they were about to leave for the second time, the elderly lady spotted the colonel's copy of the Daily Mail and grabbed it. "You've read this?" Before he could rescue his paper, she returned to the bride's side, and holding the paper above her head then began, again, the short walk to St Jaspers, keeping a watchful eye for any marauding birds.

At the church door, the unknown elderly lady threw the paper away. Jock, being more-nimble, than the colonel ran across and rescued it from the top of a tombstone. As they walked to the pub the three could hear the diminishing sound of the church organ belting out, "Here comes the bride."

The colonel later learned the wedding went ahead without a hitch. That was until the reception. Harold rarely drank alcohol, then only a glass at a time. He decided he liked the taste of champagne with its increasing calming effect on his twitching face. He was helped to the bridal bed at the Retreat where Anne managed to undress him. From the gossip, the colonel understood there were no wedding night frolics that night or the following as Harold recovered from his hangover. The bride and groom left on their honeymoon two days later.

Chapter 51

THE TRIO sat in the *Gripe and Groan* looking out of the window as the autumn rain lashed down outside. Jock commented, "D'yer realise it's nearly a year since, a year, yeah, nearly a year." He went quiet and sipped his whisky.

Lenny said, "Yeah, it's been a funny old year. Enjoyed it, really, better than being banged up."

The colonel said nothing as he scribbled some notes on an A4 notepad.

"Memory lane?" Jock ventured.

"Sort of, just remembering some of the dafter heists we were involved in and getting nicked on the job."

Lenny laughed, "Yeah, we really screwed up some blaggin's. Which one are you rememberin'?"

"I wuz think' about that Hemel Hempstead job when we surrendered to a guy dressed in green overall fings with a red beret on is 'ead 'oldin,' a pistol."

"Oh, aye, that one," Jock replied. "We only had one double barrelled sawn-off. Blew the usual 'ole in the ceilin' and wasted two cartridges, we then waited for the cashier to load the money into the holdall we gave her."

"Urgh, that job, we didn't arf get some ribbin' in chokey over that one. Remind me what 'appened', Lenny asked.

The colonel stroked his moustache and said, "Let's 'ave a refill."

He came back to the table with the barman carrying the drinks on a tray.

"This blaggin' had an embarrasin' outcome. I finks you remember how we charged into the foyer of the bank, blowin' a hole in the ceilin. In the bank, wuz a man in those green camouflage gear. We later learned he wuz a soldier and his young son was wiv 'im, dressed as a cowboy.

"The next thing we knew was he shouted at us to standstill or he's shoot us. We turned and saw his standing wiv his legs apart and pointin' a pistol at us, he shouted 'Military Police, surrender, or I'll fire." We stood still lookin' at him and, you Lenny, slowly put yer shooter down and we all raised our hands. Nicked on the job we were.

Jock laughed, "Yeah, but it wasn't so funny when we discovered the pistol was a toy one and part of the boy's cowboy rig. As I remember, the press had a field day when the fact came out at our trial."

The colonel replied, "Yeah, I seem to remember one headline said, 'Toy gun thwarts robbers'. Another said summit like, 'Robbers surrender to young cowboy'. At least we got a mention on Breakfast Tele'.

"What I remember wuz we were on remand when the prison guards let us, with others, watch tele, our names weren't mention but everyone knew it wuz us when that soldier dressed in uniform and his little son rigged up in his cowboy gear were interviewed in the studio. He wuz allowed to fire the cap gun. We got our names in the papers a couple of months later and one paper ran the headline along with our pictures, I fink it said summit like, 'Oldest bank robbers in town get jailed', underneath was a smaller line which said, 'Caught by mini-cowboy and toy pistol'."

Lenny looked at his empty glass and said, "I took a lot of stick over that, they called me a real idiot for fallin' for a toy gun."

"Never mind, Lenny, worst things can 'appen at sea'." Jock sank the last of his pint, picked up the two other glasses and headed for the bar to buy refills.

Lenny looked puzzled, "What does he mean colonel? What's does he mean?"

The colonel ignored the question as Jock sat down and gave them their pint refills.

"I think if I sexed the story up a bit I'll make it part of my speeches and me book," the colonel added.

"Okay, but what does he mean abart the sea," Lenny demanded.

"The ship could have sunk with us on board," the colonel replied.

"But we never used a ship," Lenny replied.

Jock changed the subject and asked, "I wonder what has happened that nutty prof and that woman? Neither had been seen for some time."

No one answered.

Chapter 52

THE TRIO were used to dealing with oddball situations at the Retreat. The colonel and Lenny were on their way to the *Gripe & Groan*. Jock was in a costume rehearsal at the St Jasper's church hall.

On the way, they couldn't understand what the noise was. It was alien to them. Then they heard voices shouting, "Get out', go away." The strange noise intensified.

As thy reached the main road and prepared to cross it to the pub, they were met by a group of people waving their arms at many brown and white cows in front gardens, consuming various plants and munching some long grass on a lawn. Traffic had come to a halt with lorry drivers and motorist all trying to persuade the cows to move.

The problem appeared to be their liking for garden plants and what appeared to be their pleasure of causing chaos. The bellowing seemed to be their gesture of defiance towards the human audience.

The colonel and Lenny paid for their drinks and decided to sit outside and watch the chaos as several police cars arrived. The sight of the Boys in Blue made no difference to the herd calmly devouring householder's prize geraniums, tips of rose bushes and trim the lawns.

Ayrshire cows are often called quiet and calm. They took no notice of the fuss they were causing as they meandered from one garden to another.

A man they only knew by sight commented, "Don't know why they're complainin', they're getting the muck for free."

The colonel and Lenny weren't quite sure what this meant.

As Lenny went inside the pub, Jock appeared in full highland regalia and carrying his bagpipes. He put his pipes down and went inside to get a 'wee dram'. He came out as the farmer arrived on his quad bike. He failed to persuade 35 brown and white bovines to retreat away and return to the farm.

Jock took a large sip of his drink and without saying anything, strode up the road making his way through the cows and the traffic, he acknowledged the farmer and began playing his pipes. Every one of the cows raised their heads, turned and looked up the road as Jock strode towards the farm. The herd started to follow him.

To everyone's amusement, they marched along, two at a time, like a military unit. They didn't break ranks until they filed into the field they had escaped from earlier.

Ten minutes later, the farmer arrived back with Jock sitting on the back of his quad bike. The farmer went to the bar and returned with a tray of drink for the thio and himself.

The colonel raised his glass, "Here's to Jock, the pied piper of Bogwash."

Lenny looked baffled and asked, "What's that?" No one answered him.

Chapter 53

SITTING in his flat scribbling notes about his blagging career, with Minnie asleep beside him, the colonel was remembering those who made himself and the others look brilliant with their stupidity. He thought he couldn't talk about the industry without giving them a mention.

Jimmy 'Joker' Jackson, Ahmed 'Crazy' Khan and Pete 'Plonker' Price were better known to the Federation and law enforcement as the 'Tooting Tossers'. He wrote, 'By the time we knew about 'em they had carried out a couple of heists of South London general stores and had been banged-up twice for short periods for their efforts. In both cases their haul had been packets of Weetabix, bottles of lemonade and a large amount of various sweets. All three of 'em were nicked after early CCTV surveillance recorded them raidin' the shop then later in a nearby park eating their ill-gotten gains."

The colonel decided their idiocy was memorable and he would include in talks and his book. Minnie turned over and carried on sleeping.

The colonel muttered out loud, "Yeah, their efforts made my lot look superior in the business. I've gotta tell the world just how bad they were. 'Let me see, how best can I explain to my public about their efforts and how they finally were caught and sent down for a coupla years."

The colonel wrote, 'We were annoyed with this gang's activities, they were givin' decent robbers a bad name when they raided banks and post offices, leavin' some injured customers behind. All against our trades code of conduct.

'They were getting' away with their maverick methods, well almost. Their career came to an end with a Wandsworth, South London bank that we had lined up as a target for later in the month. They parked the Ford Granada they had stolen from a Roehampton housing estate outside the bank leaving Crazy in the driving seat and the engine runnin. If anyone remembers it was the original square bodied model.'

He was warming to the tale and scribbled down his memories of what then happened.

He went on, 'Joker and Plonker ran into the bank waving rifles around, yes, rifles, not sawn-off shotguns. This raid was on the Wednesday during Boy Scouts Bob-a-Job week. Inside the bank were six uniformed Boy Scouts and two Cub Scouts in their green outfit. They were trying to persuade the manager to give them some and get paid for it. They had reasoned the bank had plenty of money and should help them and their troop raise funds.

'Matters started to fall apart with the two heist merchants. One of the boys, aged eleven, said out loud, "They ain't real guns, the barrel ain't got a hole in the end." The rest of the troop joined in shouting, "They ain't real. They ain't real'," several times.

'This unnerved the two men who began backing away out of the front door with the two 'rifles' pointin' at the Scouts and other customers. The boys' jeering became louder.

'It later transpired that they only had one real gun, an old single barrel 12-bore shotgun. As one of the team pointed the gun at the cashiers and pulled the trigger. Nothing happened. The Scouts cries intensified.

'Outside a panda car pulled up alongside the Granada preventing Crazy from leaving the driving side. Two other cars arrived at the same time and disgorged four uniformed cops all holding truncheons. Yes, truncheons, it was in the days before fancy crime-fighting kit were issued to cops.

'They were met by two would-be robbers backing out of the front door to the chants of. "Useless, useless, fake guns, fake guns." They surrendered to the police. It was discovered that one of the 'rifles' had been made of a broom handle and parts of old chair arms and legs, all painted black.

'The real gun had jammed, and the ancient cartridge got stuck in the breach.

'They spent some time in chokey thinkin' about their stupidity. That episode improved our reputation.'

Minnie woke up and wandered to her feeding dish and with a curious throaty noise demanding food.

"Not been listernen' t'me, have you?" The colonel commented as he fed him before heading for his luncheon meeting with his two pals at the *Gripe and Groan*. As he left he said to his lodger, "I'll improve that tale when I get back. At least, it will show my fans we weren't as bad as some thought."

Minnie couldn't care, food was more important.

Chapter 54

IT was now nearly Christmas and the police were no nearer solving the mystery of the four men robbing banks and post offices. The Federation of Bank Robbers had also drawn a blank trying to find them.

Bamber was hiding away in his mother's Wiltshire home, he remained convinced that Reg Crowther was still alive and the original gang of four were behind the spate of robberies.

Anne and Harold were now married and were due back in the New Year from an around the world cruise.

Joanna saw an advert in the *Hare and Hounds* magazine for riding crop with two small leather loops attached to the end. She would add the crop to her collection of punishment tools, as a Christmas present to herself. She remained bemused why so many well-educated men deliberately muddled up their English lessons and enjoyed being punished for doing so. The pain in her arm was reduced with her thrashing fewer 'naughty men'.

The real identity of Professor Giles Galbraith eluded the Trio.

Belinda had difficulties in establishing the identity of Draper. She was also spending more time with the colonel trying to establish the identity of the geriatric bank robbers. Three mysteries to solve.

Then there was the mystery of Lenny's Saturday midday meetings. Even more puzzling was the mystery of his belief that Belinda was really the retired actress Josie Lumsden. Who is she really?

Jock was quietly accepting the attention of Martha and suggested she went with him to spend Christmas and the New Year in Edinburgh with his daughter. She accepted with glee. Others pondered over the mystery of their friendship.

The mystery of why the National Bank Robbers Federation should put so much effort in helping their archenemies–the police.

There was still no news of the missing 'Loony' professor and Celia Worthy, a mystery that would be many weeks until it was solved.

Would the second year of 'The Trio's' life at the Retreat improve. It was now the third year since serving their last prison sentence, the longest term they'd been free. It was yet to be seen if these mysteries are unravelled come the New Year.

The End

Glossary

THROUGHOUT this book you will find words that are not now in everyday use even by new members of the 'underworld' but still used by the 'old lags' involved in the heist industry. The English language can be quirky, with different words meaning the same thing. The Trio still used slang dating back to the 1960s and the 1970s. Many of these words have survived the decades, others have fallen into disuse. This ***Glossary of Terms*** will help the reader understand the meaning of many of words of the period still used by the Trio.

It is also hoped this glossary will help those whose English is not their mother tongue.

A con	A confidence trickster or the act of a confidence trick. Also, a convict.
Banged-up	Serving a prison term
Blag	To rob (see heist)
Blagging.	A robbery
Blagger	A person who robs
Bluebottles	Police
Brief	Solicitor or Barrister

Buggins turn	A person chosen for promotion by rotation rather than merit
Case, cased	Too plot, to observe, spy on
Fuzz,	Police
Grass	A police informer, also cannabis. 'Guest' of the prison service. A prisoner.
Heist	To rob, a robbery
Laff	Laugh
Nick	Police station.
Nutter	An intellectually challenged individual with strange ideas
Old Bill	Police
Old lags	Old members of the criminal underworld. Old jailed criminals
Plod,	Police
Porridge	A jail sentence
Rumbled	Caught out
Sawn-off	A shotgun with its barrel and stock shortened.
Shooter	Gun
Slammer	Prison
Smackers	Slang term for monetary payment. (ten smackers = ten pounds–ten £'s).
Snout	A police informer
Tea leave	A thief
Tooled-up	Going equipped to steal whilst carrying firearms.
Totty	Young girl
Tom	A prostitute
Wimmin	Women